VOLCANO DAYS

VOLCANO DAYS

A NOVEL BY

Brian Johnson

A Patrick Crean Book

Somerville House Publishing
Toronto

Canadian Cataloguing in Publication Data

Johnson, Brian
Volcano Days

"A Patrick Crean Book"
ISBN 1-895897-21-1

I. Title.

Design: Gordon Robertson
Cover illustration: Giraudon/Art Resource, NY
1. S0043442 RM449 Color Transp.
Magritte, René. Les Fanatiques. 1945
ARS COPYRIGHT Private Collection

Printed in Canada

A Patrick Crean Book

Published by Somerville House Publishing,
a division of Somerville House Books Limited:
3080 Yonge Street, Suite 5000, Toronto, Ontario M4N 3N1

Somerville House Publishing acknowledges the financial assistance of the Ontario Publishing Centre, the Ontario Arts Council, the Ontario Development Corporation, and the Department of Communications.

To Marni

VOLCANO DAYS

FACTS

THIS IS about the time I went crazy. What is hardest to understand is the moment of rupture itself, a quickening strangeness that began on a train taking me from Montreal to Quebec City in a blizzard, and congealed into paranoia, shiny and opaque as obsidian glass. What was I afraid of? I can recall only the most pungent images: staring into Emile's snail-black eyes as he opened his briefcase on the restaurant table to show me the revolver inside; fearing for my life as I sat like a fugitive in the bus back to Montreal, convinced that the perfumed woman in the seat behind me was a deadly combination of prostitute and assassin. It seems laughable now, but the straws of truth, the glint of ivory sliding between greased palms in the night, the horrible desires motivating gangsters and politicians—all this remains irrefutable.

I do have evidence, pages and pages scribbled in a bewildering repertoire of handwriting. I've thought of stringing them into a dark novel about the castle of death, the trap-door and the terror of the private beach. But I'm loath to make things up. I don't want to uproot my delusions from that *dreadful factual ambiguity* that underlies fear and sets a torch to the imagination. Even now, I look back on the madness with a certain loyalty, as if it contained an inviolable trust.

An event did trigger it. One March night, while I slept in Quebec City, a man went on a rampage with a bulldozer hundreds of miles to the north of James Bay and made something snap in my brain. The membrane of dreams broke all at once, bringing on panic and freefall, a flight of delirium, until the delusions finally ran out on a veil of black sand, at the base of a Sicilian volcano.

Some facts are easy. I had grown up in Toronto, where events always stayed at a safe distance, a flat city where big news was a woman swimming across the lake or a new subway line being dug. I remember taking the train to Montreal for excitement in the sixties, getting buzzed on the red banquettes of the bar car, then floating up from the station into the city and feeling the sudden warmth of the crowd, the clicking glances. We would do all the tourist things. Climb the Mountain. Eat crêpes. Go to weird nightclubs, then stare at fluorescent wads of smoked meat at 4 A.M.

During one of those field trips, a weekend escape with a friend, we had been spending hours making slow, stoned love in the afternoon with the curtains drawn when my mother phoned to say that I had lost my job. The newspaper that had just hired me in Toronto had folded. It made me more giddy than upset. None of us worried much about careers back then, and I assumed that my future would slide into place the way it always had done—which it did, when a position at the paper in Montreal fell my way. I was immersed in radical politics at the time, and after playing revolution in a city with no real movement to call its own, I felt I was finally headed for the front.

Montreal was a good place to be a reporter. It had slums that burned in winter and demonstrators who ran through the downtown in the dark and fought pitched battles with the police, chanting serious slogans like the ones in Paris. It was 1971. I was twenty years old and Quebec was the closest you could come to covering a war without leaving the country. Between the politics and the Mafia, there was always more than enough going on.

One night the Blue Bird Café burned down, killing thirty-seven people who were trapped upstairs in an overcrowded country-and-western bar with a blocked fire exit. It happened a couple of hours before deadline and the whole newsroom descended on the place. While the city screamed with sirens, I watched the wrapped bodies being carried out like loaves, then dictated one-sentence paragraphs of color from a pay phone. Later that night in the press club, the newspaper bought everyone drinks.

After midnight, when they delivered the early edition,

the city editor picked a paper off the bundle and slapped it down on the bar. He stood there admiring the front page, talking about it like it was a fish he had caught. He put a drunken arm around my shoulder and slurred into my ear that I had just covered the biggest nightclub fire in North American history, that I should be proud to be part of it because I could tell my children. Without really thinking, I spilled some cognac over the paper and struck a match. The city editor watched in uncomprehending horror as a blue flame raced across the front-page picture of a fireman shrouded by smoke. The bartender, an old colonial in a red vest, threw down a wet rag without missing a beat.

At the paper, I was viewed as an Anglo whose heart lay on the other side of St. Laurent, the street that formed the frontier between English and French, between past imperfect and future conditional. Those were days when it seemed anything could happen in Quebec. Two years earlier, after the kidnapping of the British trade commissioner, the labor minister had warned that "a wind of madness" was blowing across the province. In light of what happened to him, his words were prescient. He had no way of knowing that he would be next, that he would be found folded into the trunk of a green Chevrolet, strangled with the religious medal he wore round his neck.

By the time I got to Montreal, the adventures of the FLQ were over. But like a concentrate of red dye, a measure of its insolence had seeped into the water table of the working class. The labor movement had harnessed the forces of opposition and unions hummed like turbines in a stiffening current of Quebec nationalism. As a general strike paralyzed the public service, the leaders of labor's Common Front went to jail, raising clenched fists for the camera. In the contours of the fleur-de-lys you could begin to see glints of the hammer and sickle.

At the paper, I became the labor reporter. Secretly I belonged to a local branch of the international communist conspiracy. Reporter by day, revolutionary by night, I raced through the political spectrum by cab, covering a rally of striking aircraft workers in the morning, interviewing a politician in the afternoon, then reporting back to the Organization at night. I remember the long meetings in our drafty East End storefront, listening to Marcel's jeweled analysis unfold like blank verse. The midnight sessions beside Cléo at the light table, laying out *La taupe* with X-ACTO knives. Fiddling with Letraset borders that would crack in the cold. Pasting up the back page with a photo I had filched from the newsroom of the premier eating oysters.

I was conducting espionage on all sides at once. In my own mind, my loyalties were clear. They lay with the revolution, and with a laminated Marxism that left room for Rimbaud, psychedelic drugs, surrealism, sexual innovation, augury and the Rolling Stones. But I was also working as a company scribe in the class war, and it was opening like a flower before my eyes.

One afternoon, at the end of a press conference, the

labor minister took me aside, like a teacher after class, and asked me to stay behind. He was a wiry little man, a double-breasted Machiavellian. He had never been elected. They brought him in as a hired gun after the assassination of his predecessor.

The minister poured me a cognac without asking and told me to switch on my tape recorder. He paced and talked for more than an hour, while his aides—thugs in suits—stood stationed around the room.

He called himself *le pompier*, the fireman, and liked to issue dire warnings about what would happen if the blaze of labor unrest got too big to put out. In a way, we saw eye to eye, sharing an appreciation for apocalypse, but from opposite viewpoints. I was doing my best to fan the flames from the sidelines, and I think he was on to me. At the end of the interview, as I left his office, he gave me a coy smile and asked how my Chilean friends were doing. I asked what he meant. The labor minister said his sources had informed him I had friends around the world, in places like Chile.

What I really wanted was to blow my cover entirely. I imagined going all the way over to the other side and incinerating everything bourgeois about me. As an English Canadian intoxicated by the Latin fact, I was more than willing to dispense with whatever cultural identity I had.

I felt that even my girlfriend, who was Québécoise, expected me to do something dramatic. Cléo and I shared an apartment and slept together most nights, but we maintained our own bedrooms, divided by a wall. There were no guarantees of fidelity on either side. When women phoned for me, they would be surprised to hear her voice, but she politely took messages and passed them on. Her lovers were more discreet. I admired her independence and wanted to be just like her. Cléo, who joined the Organization before I did, used to joke that she had been assigned to seduce me.

We lived in separate worlds. She was an art student; I had a career. She refused to get involved with my friends at the paper, determined not to slip into the role of a wife. The one time she let me drag her to a function, a reception with a swan carved in ice, there was an awkward encounter with Carol, my deskmate in the newsroom. We had slept together once, playing hooky one afternoon at her place. It wasn't going to turn into anything, and I didn't tell Cléo. But I could see something pass between her and Carol when they met. Soon after, Cléo calmly announced she was leaving the party. Instead of making her way back through the crowd, she slipped out through a curtain cordoning off the end of the room. I followed, and we found ourselves facing each other in an empty ballroom stacked with chairs. No words were spoken, no accusations or apologies. Cléo never liked to talk about the relationship. She drew a hand through her dark hair, as if erasing a thought, and measured me in a level gaze that gave nothing away. I pulled her to me, and we exchanged sharp, threatening kisses. Fighting our way through our clothes, we made love standing up, balanced on each other's hardness, her body light as a swing in my hands. I wondered if we could be heard over the din of the room on the other side of the curtain.

March, 1974. On the last day of winter, I took the train through the blizzard to Quebec City. Normally, this is a train that no one takes, but the province was immobilized by strikes and snow. The roads were impassable. The airports were closed. I was trying to get to a conference of the Common Front.

Things began to go awry with riveting precision, starting with the train, which headed out in the wrong direction from the station. In a panic, I turned to a businessman reading a paper across the aisle.

"This isn't the way to Quebec City."

He pretended not to hear. Likely a civil servant.

I raised my voice. "We're going the wrong way!"

"First the train goes west," he said, as if explaining something to a child, "and then it goes east."

After letting off the Anglo commuters at a station in the West Island suburbs, the train gradually circled back. Crossing a bridge, we left the island of Montreal.

Outside the window, there was nothing but snow. You couldn't tell if the train was going backwards or forwards. It rocked suspended in the storm like a plane wrapped in cloud. A man with a trolley inched his way down the aisle, handing out lunch. I was in the last seat. As he came nearer, I hungrily counted down the sandwiches that remained. It would be close. Three left. Now two. Through the cellophane, I studied the last sandwich. It looked like ham and cheese. I could have grabbed it. Oblivious to me, the trainman handed it to the civil servant, who accepted it with a smile. When I finally got the trainman to turn around, he told me there were no more sandwiches on the train, an assertion that I quickly invested with hyperbolic significance.

In Quebec City, there were no taxis. My fellow passengers stood pressed against the glass doors of the station, studying the storm. Every now and then, someone would open a door and stumble into the white blast. Choosing my moment, I pushed against the glass, the submarine weight of wind, and headed out. I slid and scrambled up the steep hill from Lower Town, practically on all fours. It was like wading upstream in a heavy current. Hopelessly late for the revolution, I felt I would never catch up.

By the time I reached the event I was supposed to be covering, it was over.

That night I met Emile, a labor reporter at one of the French papers, for dinner at the Aquarium restaurant. It was his idea. I never liked Emile. He was an unctuous man with gray, formaldehyde skin. He reminded me of a mortician.

I watched him dissect his poached fish—separating the

white flesh with fastidious care—while he outlined his proposition. Emile wanted me to to collaborate with him on a *dossier*, an exposé of union corruption at the James Bay project. We had all heard stories about what was going on there. We knew about Malette, who enforced a union monopoly in James Bay for the American syndicates, a bull-necked man who wore gold chains and held interests in nightclubs. The corruption was an open secret, like the Mafia, but proving it was another matter.

"You have no idea what's going on up there," said Emile, leaning toward me.

"I've got some idea."

"Believe me, my friend, *tu ne peux pas savoir.*"

"So tell me."

"The corruption, it goes all the way to the top."

"To the labor minister?"

Emile smiled the smile of a pimp.

"Who are your sources?" I asked.

"I'm working with someone from *la Sûreté.*"

"The police? You're spying on the unions for the police?"

"Not spying. Collaborating."

"Why do you need me?"

"If we publish a joint *dossier*—your paper and my paper—on the same day, it will have more impact."

"I'm sorry. My principles won't let me work with the police."

"These people don't care about principles, my friend."

Emile reached down for his briefcase and placed it on the table. He gently snapped it open so I could see the gun. Lying there on top of his papers.

"What's that for?" I asked.

He leaned closer. "I'm not taking any chances with Malette."

Once again, the bacterial smile. His eyes were now glistening like leeches.

I gazed at the gun, the polished wooden handle. I wanted to touch it, to feel its weight, but Emile quickly shut the briefcase and placed it back on the floor.

"Have you received any threats?" I asked.

"Not directly. But, how should I say . . . I have been led to believe that certain facts in my possession could put me at risk."

"Facts?"

"I can't tell you any more, my friend, unless you become part of the investigation."

"I'm doing my own investigation."

"Then you might consider getting one of these," said Emile, patting the side of his briefcase.

The storm had stopped. The air was still. Walking through the slanted lanes of the Old City, I cut over to the ramparts overlooking the river. The promenade was deserted. Up ahead the fake castle walls of the Château Frontenac hotel were bathed in a garish light. As I headed toward it, I noticed a car quietly prowling along the snow-covered street behind me. It pulled abreast for a moment, and then sped off. It had tinted windows.

I spent the night in a horrid little room in a turret of the Château. My mind seethed. When I finally slept, it was like visiting someone else's sleep, a sleep crowded with waking dreams: boarding a train in a Métro station filled with water that lapped the platforms; Cléo unbuttoning her blouse in a restaurant where no one cared; skiing with a leader of the Common Front, who slid down a tube into a corridor, where he began pushing a lawnmower up and down the linoleum floor; sitting in a school auditorium while a man onstage was denounced as a communist—then watching in horror as a crimson wall opened behind him and he stepped backwards into an elevator, and rose out of sight, his eyes burning through me.

They were disconnected dreams, the kind that keep shunting in and out of sleep, but they escalated into a single well-organized nightmare. It was more of a visitation than a dream. Everyone I knew came to me in a kind of gothic cabal. They were all there—Cléo, Carol, Marcel, Gilles, the city editor, the labor minister, colleagues, family—all of them suddenly on the same side, drawing me into the same secret, their faces and voices conspiring in a cathedral fire. I woke up petrified and waited for dawn.

I walked out into a changed world. It was the first day of spring and the city was embalmed in snow. That morning everyone was acting weird. The waiter who served breakfast knew what was going on. So did the man at the newsstand. Outside it was cold and clear. I headed off to the paper's office at the National Assembly, with a growing sense that I was being followed. A block from the hotel, I turned around to see a man behind me stop and stare into a store window.

I made it to the office in the press gallery. Walker, the bureau chief, was standing over the wire machine, a coffee in his hand. He ripped off the sheet and handed it to me with a smirk.

During the night, a shop steward had gone berserk with a bulldozer on a dam site in James Bay. He had rammed generators and burned down barracks.

As I read through the terse wire copy, I pictured a construction camp carved from the boreal forest, a crowd of men standing outside in the subzero, watching the havoc, the fluorescent lights going out, the sparks from fire swirling into the dark and mixing with stars suddenly visible.

The bulldozer man had acted alone. By the time he was through, he had done $10 million damage and shut down the James Bay project, something the Cree had been trying to do for ages in the courts without success. In one night a madman had brought the whole jerry-built rigging of Quebec labor politics crashing down. Malette and the labor minister would lose their jobs. The Common Front would splinter, and the union movement would crumple under the weight of government inquiries and scandals in the press.

After I'd read the wire copy, I asked Walker if the paper was going to send me to James Bay. He said they had the story covered, that they just wanted me to get some reaction from labor.

I don't remember much of the following twenty-four hours. I attended the second day of the Common Front conference and filed quotes. I got out of a cab on the way back to the office because I thought I was being followed. I threshed through another night of disturbing but unmemorable dreams.

The next morning at the press gallery, Livingstone—a cynic in a cowboy hat who liked to do acid and read comic books while covering the legislature—handed me a copy of my newspaper. Next to the front-page piece on the James Bay sabotage was a big story slamming union corruption. Livingstone had it all marked up, underlining a half dozen references to anonymous management sources, which were the only sources in the story. He thought it was funny. As I read down the page, I was furious. I saw nothing but lies and innuendo. The contractors, the men who had been quietly bribing the unions to keep the peace, were now blowing the whistle on them. It was my beat. I was not consulted. The conspiracy was closing ranks.

It was time to act. In the thick of the biggest labor crisis in years, I dropped out of sight for several days without saying a word to my editor.

By this point I was convinced that I was being followed

by police and Mafia thugs. Doormen, taxi drivers, no one could be trusted. I picked up my things from the hotel and ran to the bus station, where I bought a ticket to Montreal. Once on the bus, for a moment I felt safe. All the circuits began to relax. Then, just before we pulled out of the terminal, a woman with heavy makeup and dark, blunt-cut hair got on the bus. Looking right at me, she slipped into the seat directly behind mine. The perfume gave her away. Cold crept up my neck as I realized that she had been hired to seduce me, or kill me. Probably both.

By the time I reached Montreal, I felt lucky to be alive. Cléo wasn't home. She was visiting a friend in Halifax. Marcel agreed to meet me at the Mazurka. He ordered a Czech pilsner and listened to my report, which he seemed to appreciate, although he expressed doubts about the woman on the bus. Marcel was not afraid to think in extremes, but no matter what was going on, he had a way of putting it in a calming perspective. He would fix you with his steady gaze (made steadier by the fact that he was blind in one eye) and carve off aphorisms. He never got tired of saying *"Il ne faut pas péter plus haut que son cul"*—You shouldn't fart higher than your asshole.

But that night he respected the gravity of my intentions. He told me the story of the singer who was herded with thousands of others into the Santiago arena during the Chilean coup, the singer who kept on singing his song of resistance even after the soldiers had broken his hands.

Marcel left me with two instructions.

He said, "A revolutionary has to maintain an outer coldness to disarm his enemies while never losing sight of the humanity that makes the whole exercise less than abstract."

He also said, "The three seconds before you intervene are very important. You have to be very careful."

I held a press conference to announce my resignation from the paper. It was remarkably well attended. Reading a communiqué in French, I denounced my newspaper for "defending the ecology of Westmount in times of calm while snapping to the side of the police state in times of crisis." I pointed to monstrous collusion between my editors and the Mafia cartel of James Bay contractors. The French reporters wanted proof. "Where is your *dossier*?" they asked. I had none. Several colleagues from my paper, including the cartoonist, who spent the press conference sketching, looked at me like someone who had just set himself on fire.

That afternoon the CBC kindly invited me onto live television for the local supper-hour news, assuming that, with my resignation, I was the one man who could unlock the terrible secrets of corruption at James Bay.

I went into makeup. Everyone treated me splendidly. Being the story was much better than covering the story. I was escorted to a seat in a large studio, and after viewers watched a capsule summary on how the media had reported the events at James Bay, the show's host gave me a momentous introduction and asked me to explain just what in the dickens was going on up there. What had I discovered that made me take such drastic action?

When I cordially told him that I would not talk about James Bay because I had stopped working for the bourgeois press, he went white. I then began to explain the complex villainy of the media as best I could, pointing out that the CBC was by no means exempt. The host, realizing that he was on live television with a guest who was stark raving mad, scrambled to get me off. Struggling to keep his face under control, he turned to the camera and said there would be a short pause for something or other. I kept on talking, and just before I was cut off, I looked out at the grinning camera crew, who seemed delighted to have someone break the monotony of the show, and said, "But what about the technicians? Don't *they* get a say in this decision?"

I walked out into the winds of Dorchester Boulevard feeling that my accomplishments had just begun. From that moment on, everything accelerated. I was in motion.

A few days later, I visited the newspaper for the first time since taking that train to Quebec City. I walked into the newsroom carrying an empty bag to clean out my desk. People stopped what they were doing and stared. As I stared back, their faces lit up with nervous smiles. They didn't know whether to buy me a drink or call the bomb squad. Carol, who covered the health beat, asked how I was with genuine concern, and I assured her that I had never felt better. She said she could find me a good doctor. Suzanne, a political reporter who smoked a lot of dope and liked to wear a buckskin blouse with no bra, told me under her breath in that quick, jittery way of hers that she knew *exactly* what I was doing and thought it was amazing. But she was a little wiggy herself.

Then Kevin, the obsequious travel editor, who had made a big deal about offering me a free trip to the island of Dominica two weeks earlier ("Black sand beaches—very offbeat"), congratulated me on my idealism with a frozen smile.

"But I guess that nixes the trip," he said. "It's a pity. I think you would have found Dominica fascinating."

"Not half as fascinating as where I am now."

After clearing some things out of my desk, I strolled over to the composing room, bag conspicuously in hand. I felt I was wearing a magnetic field that scoured the walls as I walked. One of the editors followed me.

"So I guess now you're going to tell us you've got a bomb in there," he said with a disingenuous laugh.

"It's not that kind of revolution," I said.

Kevin and Frank, the assistant city editor, casually joined me as I entered the composing room. They didn't know I was just crazy. For all they knew, I could be dangerous. I was a recent immigrant from Toronto, but these people were English Montrealers, born and bred; they had the sort of hair-trigger sensitivity to these things that comes from growing up in neighborhoods with exploding mailboxes.

Looking around the composing room, I felt a giddy sense of power, a tingling invincibility that surged through my skin and seemed to charge the air in the room.

The lights went out. The machines went silent. Kevin and Frank exchanged panicked looks, then followed as I walked back into the newsroom. It, too, was blacked out.

"I suppose you did this," said Frank, only half joking.

I didn't say anything. I just smiled and left the building, looking forward to playing some harmonica in the underpass on the way home.

I had all the confirmation I needed.

BELIEFS

I COULD give you more facts. But it's not by timidly patting around the grave of experience that I can achieve my goal, which is neither analysis nor conclusion but a reunion with the current of ecstasy that put coincidence in command and turned the impossible into a stroll down the street. The terror of *conscious, orchestrated decay*, and the suspicion that there was nothing else at work than an allegiance of diabolical forces united against my movements—this was like a dust storm raging through my freshly liberated imagination.

It wasn't long before I took the next unconscious maneuver in my rush to escape the world-as-we-know-it and thrust myself behind the eye of history. I went backstage. I transformed all sensory impression into a conspiracy of pleasure. A delirious turncoat, I swung from paranoia to ecstasy—from crouching, babbling cowardice to naive experiments at being a god. It was like having the imagination of a child and the mental technology of an adult.

Time was my first victim. As I wrote in my diary: "Time was the first friend whose smiling dead lips turned bloody and moved. Numbers became flirtatious digits to be enjoyed rather than compiled. There was no question about the truth: it was whatever key enlightened all the electrical circuits at the same moment." For several days, I listened to the radio, convinced that my nervous system was acting not only as an antenna but as a co-transmitter. Clocks and radios became toys, elastic bands with which I would test my psychic powers. Tweaking the radio dial in a specific way, I could snap the airwaves like a towel and send kinks and warbles back the other way. I could get inside an announcer's head until he was practically calling me by name (which was not all that unusual in the days of underground FM, when broadcasters made their heads so available). I believed in the subjective inversion by which I anticipated events. The phone would ring on cue. I was convinced that I could make things happen simply by thinking about them. But the price I paid for this secret and enormous power was total marginality in the world of belief, business and politics.

Walking the streets, I endowed the anarchic organization of traffic with harmony, structure and direction. In any mass of people circulating on the sidewalks downtown, there was always an implied rainbow. And through sheer intuition, I could chart my way to a buried treasure of marvels. I gauged my social movements to a color scheme in which clothing, automobiles and traffic lights all acted as warnings or enticements, indicators of whether I should nurture or censor my fantasy of the moment. The color in which I found safety and personal identity was burnt orange. That color wasn't just a symbol. I thought it was directly equivalent to the rate at which I was burning up in the atmosphere. It set my speed limit. Blue was identified with repression. It triggered an instant signal to slow down and watch out. Blue's opposite number, red, indicated revolution and danger—it, too, was a signal to slow down for safety's sake, but also a seduction to enter a newer, faster phase of contestation. Burnt orange was like advanced adolescence. When it passed over into red, it produced a state of war. The war is always going on. The fighting takes place on the perimeter, a world of high winds and sirens, while we are huddled around the music.

Black, of course, represented death in all its endless intrigue. A stark cosmic event, morally undistinguished and politically neutral. I began to see things from the viewpoint of black rather than white, which produced some interesting optical reversals. In focusing on sharp contrasts through a camera lens, I felt I could produce combustion through sheer visual concentration. This delusion included the smell of smoke. The same day that I discovered that my eyes could induce arson, I had a dreadful premonition that the arts school where Cléo was working would be blown to bits by a bomb placed on the construction site beside it. The arts school overlooked the construction site, like a balcony over the pit, and there was a countdown painted by students on the blue hoarding around the site: "5 . . . 4 . . . 3 . . . 2 . . . 1 BANG." This graffiti, combined with an official blast warning from the construction company, was enough to spark my premonition. It was also May 1, May Day, and I could feel the low crackling of civil war in all the hard surfaces of the city. Cléo was working on a sculpture, a woman's head in clay, which she kept wrapped in wet rags, but it kept drying out faster than she could finish it. I had visions of artists drawing fuses out of the ground like tree roots and slicking them down with paint, while the workers lost their patience and prepared to blow the whole thing sky high.

All these events on the verge of ignition filled my brain like a phosphorous bath. Writing became a lifeline, the wriggling spell of ink still wet on the page. I threaded my way through the static with semaphore manifestos:

"Who has the patience for prose, for systematic recollection of lost water? Who has time to string and sew pearls while new stars are being born this very instant? . . .

"Poetry is never the product of illusion or artifice, but the dangerous and beautiful *act* of seeing something imagined thus real. Poetry, as printed residue of psychic combustion, is not grounds for insanity, even though certain states do repress poets for the seditious weight of their thoughts. But both poetry and delusion require a willed displacement of consciousness to frontiers of the human psyche where seeing is a risk and believing is a sin. . .

"For the poet and the madman, confirming the reality of the dream is essential: i.e., bringing back pictures. There's no point defying gravity, stepping blindfolded through the looking glass, or freefalling through King Solomon's mines, if you can't bring something back—at least a story, if not precious stones and a totem. The trick is getting them through customs, across the quarantine line that separates the safe from the insane. Mad delusion and artistic rampage both involve the transformation of the mind from satellite dish to ray gun. Through perceptual inversion, we transform reality with desire, and while this perceptual inversion does not get the same recognition as *con*version, the poet and the madman would have it otherwise . . .

"It is not enough that society's glass eye and digital clock join forces to conclude that what we have before us is a lunatic, whose lunacy is due to the moon, whose influence we should censor. Maybe. But that delirious vision, in which we see only what we most desperately want to see, still wants to be seen. The vision itself melts memory and perception into a single bolt of mercury. For the poet—and the madman—confirming the vision (minting the delirium) is essential not for the intrinsic value of the pearls that can be hurled down the gob of empiricism, but for survival. The bourgeoisie confuses baubles, symbols and concessions with art. In the art market, the pearls are all that count. The pearl diver's blacked-out dream is written off as just so much overhead, while capitalism decks itself in buried treasure. 'Art' becomes a clanking wardrobe of chain mail and sequins. The artist has to turn the dream into product only for social and psychic survival. Otherwise he is a lunatic. But the finished work is never more than a pale shadow of what suggested it, and has value only insofar as it defies possession. We need paintings that spit . . .

"The secret of art, the one that refuses to be consumed or marketed, is the act of forging prophecy out of premonition. The artist and the madman join in the dance of projectiles, an activity that allows certain psychic privileges. This is not a theatrical game of 'let's pretend,' but a fanatical belief in the connection between dreams and gunshots miles away."

During those early day of May, when I could feel the blush of revolution in every warming breeze, I was alone. Cléo, who had immersed herself in making a student film of her friend's aquarium, kept her distance, and I was so busy that I hardly noticed. We agreed that when the dust settled, we would see each other on the other side.

One evening Marcel summoned me to the Mazurka and confided in all seriousness that Montreal was getting too hot for me. He said I would be more valuable to the comrades in Toronto, where I could provide a first-hand analysis of the situation in Quebec. At the time, I didn't know that I was being humored. The Organization had no idea what to do with me, and because I had come from Toronto in the first place, they thought it best to send me back there for a while and let its branch serve as an asylum: a cell padded with Marxism.

But, as I prepared my departure, all I knew is that I was back in motion, a vector running interference through the folds of the system. All around me the system was overheating, blinking with warning lights at every turn, and as I gathered velocity, I reacquired the focus of a fugitive. I had to escape the city at all costs. I could feel it sealing up behind me. The planes were all grounded by a strike of air-traffic controllers. Wildcat walkouts had shut down most of the downtown telephone exchanges. To make some phone calls, I "occupied" a private office at a bank branch in Place du Canada, staying twenty minutes past closing time—finally arousing the indignation of a senior official, who ordered me out. I told him I needed some cash first. Hovering behind the teller, he nervously supervised my withdrawal. When he told me that he was the manager, I gave him an incredulous look and assured him he was doing a fine job.

FEAR

THE POWER that rips up years of masking tape and flings your mind into the fire does so blindly. In Toronto I was hanging by my fingernails from a death mask, deepening the creases under my father's eyes. I arrived in a fever, convinced I was as hot as an escaped convict, and ran through the streets crouched and clutching my shirt like a demon. I would prefer to skip forward and tell you about the ecstasy, the prophecies that actually came true, the satin shirt, the magnetic movements of the sea before dawn, the incestuous implications of music, the collision between the garden and the wall, the arrow and the fish, the fire and the mountain, the insects and their keepers . . . Yet I feel compelled to pick apart that hysterical trip to Toronto, because it was the lowest point of my insanity.

Arriving at the station too late to get on any of the fast trains, I ended up on what seemed like a heavily policed cattle car. I scribbled feverishly in my diary—mostly nonsense—to ward off fear. As we pulled out of Montreal, I wrote:

"On the corner seat sits a Motorola radio like the kind cops use. It is someone's property, so it is probably very sensitive. I feel the cold creeping up my throat. I have to move. The nattering is full strength on the Motorola. When I move, it starts; when I stop, it stops. The radio is insane . . ."

I saw the train as an institution. And I wandered up and down asking the trainmen if I could find a French newspaper. I threw a tantrum, in French, in the first-class car and demanded to see the conductor. A trainman pointed me toward the rear of the train. Following his directions all too literally, I walked back through the carriages, until I ended up in the caboose, or some sort of mail car. In the middle of it was a woodstove, a dog and a fresh copy of the Montreal *Star*. Determined to keep going until officialdom directed me otherwise, I crawled over the mailbags that were piled several feet high at the end of the caboose. I resisted the temptation to rip one open and read my final instructions.

Trains, like ships, are full of little knobs and levers and doors, all bearing bureaucratic signs saying what you can do with them and what the fines are for misusing them. This final message on the back door of the baggage car was stenciled and terse. No fines. No laws. Only a simple instruction about how to open the door. Given the lack of

French-language newspapers on the train, I thought a fair revenge would be to lift the latch and let the Royal Mail go spilling onto the tracks. The event would be supremely comic, I thought, confident that the instructions on the door would render my act quite legal.

Then the man in charge of the baggage car arrived and asked me what the hell I was doing. "Get down from there," he shouted. I got down, silent as a camel, and explained the obvious: "I was looking for the conductor." When that failed to satisfy him, I delivered a strongly worded but diplomatic indictment of the lack of francophone reading material on the train. The man was unsympathetic, to say the least.

The train stopped. The caboose doors slid open. Outside it was cold and black, a small station in the middle of nowhere, two men with cowboy hats and cruel faces. The trainman tossed some bags to them and stepped out to talk. I was suddenly afraid, trapped behind enemy lines in a civil war, fighting for the French language on a midnight train in the middle of Ontario. The trainman threatened to kick me off the train and hand me over to the police. But instead I was quarantined in a red car and told not to move. Two girls in red cheerleader sweaters sat beside me. I assumed they were police.

Later they put me in a regular car beside a crippled woman who had yellow hair and pallid skin and talked like death. The train stopped somewhere. No one knew why. It was a twilight-zone moment where you fear that time will freeze and you will never arrive and like that you die.

By the time the train reached Toronto I was so far behind enemy lines I was breathing in code. Fortunately, the city was locked in a trance. I slipped out of the station unnoticed and took a cab to Martin's house in Cabbagetown. He was a member of the Organization's Toronto affiliate, and one of Cléo's ex-lovers. That night I didn't sleep. My mind raced with agendas.

I spent a productive afternoon writing poetry with a tiny brush dipped in red Gestetner fluid, the kind used to correct mimeograph stencils. For my canvas I chose a freshly painted expanse of white wall by the foot of the stairs. When Martin came home and saw my work, he tried to repress his reaction, as if nothing could surprise him. But you could see the rage get bottled up in his square, solid face, in the curl of his lip and the italic-bold eyebrows, which daggered up at the corners at the best of times and were now poised like exclamation marks. He wouldn't even look at me. He just kept shaking his head and saying, "Fucking great, this is fucking great." Then he picked up the phone and tried to call someone, who wasn't in. I tried to humor him, but he was beyond help. He simply refused to appreciate the immaculate subversion of red poetry masking white property, of words transcending walls.

In Toronto, I stayed up for days, running a fever and more convinced than ever that I was a revolutionary artist in a city of the damned, a foreign agent in a place where superstition had lulled the population into a humorless sleep. Friends from the Organization took turns sheltering me. The women were the most understanding, and the most fun. None of them had children, and they treated their time with me like child care, a domestic chore that held some potential for magic.

Dorothy took me shopping. While she bought wine at the liquor store, I asked the sales clerk for a rag and proceeded to dust the plastic grapes. They needed it. Back at the house, as Dorothy scrubbed a wooden cutting board and told me how microbes could get trapped in the wood, I explained to her how the simple circuitry of electric appliances formed a state-controlled surveillance grid that modulated our brain waves. "Transistors," I said, "are the synapses, the intelligence posts. *Solid state*—think about it." I pointed out that there was no way of avoiding the electromagnetic influence completely—*I'm not a utopian*—but it helped to keep the circuits distinct. Keep the wires separate, straight and parallel; *and don't let the toaster anywhere near the radio.*

Nighttime was the worst. That's when all the circuits combined to form a passive, unified network, an endless antenna that hummed down through our cellophane layers of sleep, imprinting dreams. I discovered that the safest place was the bath. At Dorothy's, I got into the bath at five and stayed there for the rest of the morning, holding court. Visitors came to see me, each hoping to solve the riddle that I had come to represent. But after I had entertained their questions, they all left reasonably satisfied that I posed no danger to myself or others. Valerie even gave me her silk scarf.

For hours I lay suspended in an impenetrable calm, my skin buffered by fragrant oils. I studied the waterline wincing away from the shoals where my body creased the surface. People came in and out: the curious, the therapeutic, the concerned. I received them like a reclining Buddha.

The phone rang. Through the door, which was ajar, I could hear Dorothy's voice:

"He's in the bath. Should I ask him to call you? . . . I don't think that's a good idea . . . But, Cléo, he's *happy* in the bath. I've never seen him so relaxed . . . I'm sorry, Cléo, I don't think he's in any state to talk to you. He's too sensitive . . . Well, I'll ask him. But you have to promise not to . . . Okay, hold on."

Dorothy put down the phone and came in.

"It's Cléo."

"Can you bring the phone in here?"

"It won't reach. You'll have to get out."

Dorothy got a bathtowel out of the cupboard. I stood up slowly, brushing off the soap bubbles in a careful pattern. Standing up after all this time made me feel very tall.

"Here, I'll rinse you off," said Dorothy. She unhooked the shower attachment and ran the spray up and down my body. She was brisk and efficient, like a mother. As the water glanced across my genitals, they flowered slightly to the touch.

"That's nice," I said.

She laughed. "Put this on and get the phone." She wrapped the towel around me.

The receiver lay off the hook on Dorothy's desk. I stared at it until it didn't look like a phone anymore. Then I heard Cléo's voice, sounding tiny, as if it were trapped inside.

I picked it up.

"*Salut,* Cléo."

"*Finalement!* What's going on there?"

"I was in the bath."

"So I heard. Was Dorothy in the bath too?"

"No. She's been busy aligning the co-ordinates. Why do you sound so far away?"

"I am far away. Why are you acting so crazy?"

"I'm not. You have no idea what it's like here."

"I got a frantic call from Martin. He said you'd scribbled all over his walls."

"C'mon, you know Martin. He doesn't know the first thing about art."

"But you can't go around writing on walls."

"It was just the one wall."

"People keep calling me, expecting me to *do* something about you."

"What do you tell them?"

"Nothing. I tell them I'm not responsible for you."

"Good."

"When are you thinking of coming back to Montreal?"

"I'm not thinking. I *refuse* to think. *Montréal, mon réal, mon réel. Il n'y a rien de réel à Toronto.*"

"*Arrête.*"

"You don't know what it's like here. *Ici j'suis comme une balle de caoutchouc indien, une molécule superchargée . . .*"

"*Ecoute, faut faire attention.* If you go too far, you might not come back. You have to control yourself."

"I've never felt more in control of myself."

"You know what I mean."

"*Fais-toi z'en pas.* I know what I'm doing."

"Well, nobody else does, so be careful."

"Okay, I'll see you when I get back."

"Maybe."

"Maybe?"

"I need to spend some time alone. I can't deal with you now."

"Dorothy's just turned the radio on. Everything's going to get out of phase. I've got to go, but I'll phone you right back."

"No. Write me a letter."

"You're right. That'll be safer."

"Bye bye."

"*Salut.*"

Dorothy told me I was being moved back to Martin's place. He would be spending the nights with his girlfriend down the street, so his room was free. I had to promise to keep the walls clean and not burn the place down.

One morning I set out to buy a pound of butter and a copy of *The Exorcist.* I searched through the paperback stands in several neighborhood stores but couldn't find the book. This, I thought, was a supreme injustice, that such a highly publicized book was unavailable. I walked into a store and said, "I'm looking for a book, a very famous book." But I wouldn't name it. My clues multiplied into an elaborate game of charades in which two children took an active role until one of them guessed the title. Storekeepers kept referring me to "the store down the street." Finally I found a used-book shop. I stalked the aisles, picking up books I considered grossly objectionable, reading quotations at random to punctuate an impassioned speech about ideological smut, and slamming the books down on the counter one after the other. The speech gained intensity with each volume I picked up. I singled out pop paperbacks on the identity of communism and fascism, that sort of thing. An old woman with the air of a religious fanatic eyed me with interest, as a kindred spirit. Finally I approached the storekeeper and, politely, asked if he didn't have a copy of *The Exorcist.* He didn't. I returned to the house for breakfast, clutching my coat, shivering with fear and growling at passers-by as if I had just escaped.

I was quite taken by the Chinese in the corner grocery stores. They struck me as exceptionally cool, eyes and fingers darting like lightning across an infinite web of families and clans, all bound together by a super-conductive dark green fluid. A Chinaman behind the cash at one of my *Exorcist* stops seemed immensely entertained by my act, which could have been a fireworks display or a puppet show.

After several nights of no sleep, I was getting quite demented, and my friends insisted I sleep even if it meant taking a pill. That made me even more paranoid. I wondered why people wanted to put me to sleep, and imagined, if I complied, that I would never wake up. I spent a long hysterical evening alone cleaning the kitchen and the bathroom at Martin's house, hallucinating on the mysteries of light and dark, clean and dirty, healthy and sick, alive and dead. I spent hours on my hands and knees literally shepherding germs into the garbage, envisioning each speck of dirt as some distant cousin of the bubonic plague, part of a vast continuum that had to be traced back to its earliest roots. While I cleaned, my mind threshed at a furious pace. It had great plans for a book, an epic novel. Opening sentences ticked over, plots and themes were visible for miles ahead. But, morally bound to resist instant gratification, I deferred the urge to write. Suffer. Learn. Don't let your mind slobber all over the first idea it finds. My imagination became a monastery, hypersensitive to the slightest disturbance or discovery. I decided to follow my fears to the end.

Finally I crawled off to bed in that third-story room with the peaked roof, gothic desk and big red quilt. Beside the bed was a space heater, which worked by thermostat. It seemed to go on and off in relation to my brain waves, like a cat. To make it glow I thought warm thoughts. This device did a lot to nourish my convictions about the implicit link between my psychic energy and the currents of gas, water, fire, electricity, germs and so on that were bottled up and squeezed along a circuit of conduits throughout the city. In touch with the world by electromagnetic whiplash, I could both receive and transmit radio waves. I sent off a ghostly shadow that made dogs howl.

I put the radio on my lap—interpreting the center of the red bedspread. The wires must be straightened out. Can't have these things curling every which way, crossing each other, confusing the lines of communications. Must find out where they lead. Expedition to the floor. I have nothing to fear. The light is out, but my fingers are like a thousand eyes. They touch the wire of the heater and slowly slide along its insulated length. I am open to all sensations. If I follow the wire in blind obedience to my senses, objective chance will lead me to the truth. The wire disappears under the bed. Lying on my stomach, I bend my hand under the bed, following the wire. Suddenly I stop. My fingers are touching something furry, small. A rabbit's foot. I've discovered a rabbit's foot. Seek and ye shall find. The rainbow lives up to its hype. My destiny leads to breadfruit. I have humbled myself and grown richer. But wait. The fur is warm . . . the fur is wet. I panic and look under the bed, and lying in the dim light I see the dark, sick, dead body of an animal. A mouse, a rat. I scream. The house is infected.

In fear, I put my hand to my mouth. No! Not the hand that touched *it*! The hand that felt the warm wet sick dead rat is now spreading the plague across my lip in an orgy of chemical tingling. I remove my hand as if I had touched a hot iron and run downstairs, feeling my lip blister with disease. I look in the bathroom mirror. Sure enough, on the spot where I had touched it with the mouse-hand, a small blister has formed and is growing before my very eyes. I rummage through the medicine chest but find nothing. So, with the grimace of a soldier plucking a bullet out of his leg with a penknife, I set out to clean the lip. Soap, water, tissue paper. Careful. Keep it confined to a small area. Don't spread the germs. Lacking a disinfectant to soothe the burning, I apply some toothpaste, which is remarkably cold and white.

I phone Martin, who is around the corner sleeping with his girlfriend, and beg him to take the creature away. Expecting something larger, he arrives with a shovel, this sullen earth figure who could have been an undertaker, an exorcist, or the devil himself.

At the end of a sleepless vigil I stepped, acquitted, into a spotless dawn. There were miracles wherever I walked. I heard wet grass prickling under the sun. I watched a milk truck pull up beside a graveyard, with the new tires gleaming licorice black. I loved the mornings.

PARTICLES

A DELUSION from the journal: "Looking east out of Martin's window at dawn, through rainbow halos around my breath, I can make babies cry and dogs bark. I can make the raccoon come down the chimney. I can blow the white roof off the dome beside the hall of justice."

The raccoon is an animal that came into my parents' suburban home uninvited. I felt a twinge of brotherhood with this creature as soon as my father had mentioned him to me on the phone. Its intrusion coincided with my own. The raccoon was truth and sexuality incarnate; he was my ally, my surrogate. The raccoon brings the cosmos into the living room. He brings the smell of death. We never had animals in our house, not even dogs.

I spent my childhood obsessed with safe pursuits. I devoured war stories. My favorite was about Douglas Bader, who kept getting his legs shot off. I thought getting shot down was one of the finest things that could happen to you. Hearing the big German boots crunch through the snow, waiting for the thud of a bullet in your back. *Thud*, that's how they talked about it, these prisoners of war tunneling out of the camps or trekking across the Finn frontier with gangrene spilling from their skiboots. *Thud*, like a hymn book closing.

When I wasn't reading, I would happily spend hours in the furnace room with my collection of rocks and minerals—testing for hardness and cleavage, numbering specimens with India ink. I loved the names: cinnabar, obsidian, sardonyx, molybdenite, hornblende, feldspar. My favorites were the black tourmaline crystals. I was also quite fond of two large chunks of asbestos that my father had brought back from a business trip to Quebec, rocks banded with silver fur, like sealskin, that could be shredded with a fingernail.

Later I got bored with rocks and moved on to ham radio. To get a transmitting license, you had to study circuitry. I learned to love the waxy yellow capacitors, the brown resistors striped with color bars. Hunched over a trestle table in the basement, I divined my way through the shortwave band on a war-surplus rig designed for Russian tanks. I twirled Bakelite knobs with Cyrillic labels and tapped Morse code to middle-aged nerds in North Carolina who talked about the weather.

I was, in short, no trouble as a kid. Not even as a teenager. Which must have made my sudden change in behavior at the age of twenty-five seem that much more alarming to my loving parents. During my mission in Toronto, I showed up one Sunday night for dinner. I wasn't hostile. On the contrary, I was looking for an exceptionally honest intimacy. Over roast beef, I informed my mother and father that I could no longer relate to them as a couple. From now on, I wanted to treat them as individuals, and find out who they were before they met. They treated me gingerly, as if I had been recently abducted by aliens.

After dinner, I made a pilgrimage to the basement, past the chiming grandfather clock at the top of the stairs. I looked around the rec room full of artifacts: the pewter plates, the stuffed baby alligator crawling up the wood paneling, my Plasticine map of Canada that Father had framed so meticulously under glass, the globe lamp with the cold brass nude at the base that I had caressed with so much imagination as a child.

I went into the furnace room. Still there, hanging from a peg rack on the wall, was the small prospector's pick I had used for collecting rocks and minerals. The head of the pick had a square hammer at one end, painted red. The other end tapered to a sharp chisel. My name was carved in the wooden handle. With great reverence, I brought the pick upstairs and gently placed it on the polished walnut table in the hall. My father, who watched me from behind his newspaper in the living room, looked gravely concerned. My mother came out from the kitchen and asked, a little too cheerily, why I had brought that thing up from the basement. I said it was a long time since I'd seen it.

They must have been terrified. Wondering if I was going to split their skulls open. I didn't have the slightest inclination to do anything of the kind. I was never violent. But I think it occurred to me at the time, on some slyly conscious level—and this is the one thing I still regret—that they might be drawing a darker impression. And I did nothing to dispel it. I was too pleased by the fetish magic that my old hammer had suddenly acquired simply by virtue of being moved out of the basement. As I left the house that night, I studied the moths circling the light above the garage door, weaving sinister orbits, and wondered what the raccoon was up to.

The next day, my parents put in a call to my brother, who worked in Rome as an economist for an agency that I suspected was a cover for anti-communist espionage. He tried to reassure my parents about my condition by telling them it was caused by LSD. When I told my brother that I was not doing drugs, that I had not needed drugs since leaving the paper, he believed me at once. But he insisted that our parents would be better off if they could attribute my behavior to acid, which he had described as relatively harmless. LSD, he said, would explain things. My brother, who seemed to have my best interests at heart, also urged me to take an Italian vacation.

From time to time, of course, I did drop acid. It was for special occasions. The drug did not amplify the delusions so much as give me microscopic insights into their musical structure. Every trip I took brought back a particular refrain of sounds that were identical each time. I thought if I could only decipher them, I could come up with a kind of subatomic horoscope. Flooding up from my preconscious, this code of sounds from the inside came accessorized with textures and odors. It was just there, a persistent chant fluxing through the cells, like crickets on a summer night, like plankton buzzing light into the surf—consciousness as percussion against the reef of memory.

The acid sounds drumming up from the depths worked precisely, as tumblers opening and closing space. Ball-bearings on velvet, the smack of billiards, Chiclets, molecules . . . molecules, that's what Cléo thought was happening. She said the chemical triggered an atomic avalanche in the brain.

On acid, you can smell the combustion of your own skin.

What's that taste in your mouth? Me.

The body becomes as objective as anything else, as damp as the earth, as susceptible as the sea.

Acid issues a special license to the imagination, a short-term infinity permit.

But my most exaggerated acts of delusion were committed in a state of strict sobriety. They were dictated by a super-conscious, almost military sense of strategy. The acid trips served as time-outs; they were the therapy sessions.

The madness, the brain fever, was ignited by an overdose of rationality, an incandescent state of sober second thought. It begins with an overheated differential between the subjective and objective worlds—between the I and the It, the self and the shelf. The crazed mind revs and revs, looking for torsion. When it finally connects, it bites into reality like a ratchet, generating more friction and more fever, until the whole synaptic gearbox is stripped.

A fault had opened up in my psyche, a rift between the world out there and the one in here. But on acid the boundary between the subjective and objective simply dissolves. The wind goes right through you. As body and mind merge in a molecular stream, the whole notion of controlling the world (the paranoid mind's political conceit) is rendered absurd. My experience may not be typical, but for me acid was the Great Equalizer, a window with a good light by which I could watch the pieces of my reconfigured sanity click into place.

I did not act crazy on acid. There was no need to. There was always so much to observe, so much detail to account for, that taking extravagant action seemed beside the point. For me, LSD clarified all the ABCs of sensory processing, including logic: it heightened rationality. My acid trips were luxurious, but absurdly sane. In the evolutionary progress of my madness, they were the bean-counting sessions. Each trip was a kind of audit, an occasion to demagnetize the mind and start fresh. A chance to reformat the software.

On LSD, I didn't lose my marbles; I played with them.

"Drugs" and "madness," of course, are loaded terms. Both are tinged with illegality. Conventional wisdom would assume that acid triggered the madness, whereas it had more to do with its "cure"—another loaded word, considering that the madness was itself a kind of cure.

It was my matriculation ceremony. The well-mannered Wasp who came to Canada at the age of five with a beveled English accent, the sweetly obedient boy who kept his pajamas folded crisply under his pillow and knelt beside the bed to say his prayers—he grew up to discover blacks, Jews, injustice, Vietnam and vaginal discourse. Marx and sex both ended in *x* and intersected in Quebec, a country within a country that (as Charlebois noted) begins with a Q and ends with a *bec*, a kiss. I embraced Quebec as my Magnificent Other. I threw myself at her feet, pledging to burn all the bridges that took me there.

In my mind's eye, Toronto became the enemy, the home and native fatherland that would never understand. During my homecoming, I took perverse revenge on my past, then returned to Montreal in triumph, more convinced than ever that I was on the right track.

The train ride was smooth and uneventfully pleasant. But this time, of course, I wasn't going against the grain. Going back to Montreal was always easier. All the forcefields were congruent, drawing me out of the Ontario flatland, toward the city that lies curled like a cat around the Mountain. I could feel the accelerating warmth as the train crossed the bridge to the island of Montreal, then shuffled up to the downtown through the tenements of Lachine and St. Henri, finally slipping into a hole under Place Bonaventure. Then the cab. The twang of joual. The centrifugal speed of the traffic.

I wondered if Cléo would be there. We had talked on the phone before I left. But with everyone calling her for advice on what to do with me, she was not really in the mood for commitment. She said she had spent the week in monastic silence, working on the short film for the art school, *Soluble Fish.*

When I got home, she was sitting cross-legged on the bed, in jeans and a T-shirt, reading a book. Her hair was different. It was still dark, but cropped short with glints of copper and spiky edges. The gamine body, and now the hair. She looked more androgynous than ever, except for the mouth. Her full lips had always struck me as defiantly female.

"You've changed," I said, sitting across from her on the bed.

"I thought it was time to be somebody else."

"And who might that be?"

"Ah, wouldn't you like to know?"

"You're like a stranger."

"Look who's talking—*l'architecte de l'abandon.* So. Are you back now, or are you still out there?"

"Both."

Cléo raised an eyebrow and conceded a smile. We looked at each other in silence, sensing electricity in the new distance between us. She lit a cigarette. I traced a fingertip along her collarbone. She was wearing a new necklace, a coil of Indian silver half-hidden by her shirt.

"Where's this from?"

"It was a gift."

"Who from?"

"A friend."

I didn't pursue it. There was a thrill in not knowing who she was or where she'd been. Or if we were still lovers. Kneeling, I placed my hands around her waist, under her shirt.

"Why don't you take this off," I said. "So I can see the necklace against your skin."

"That's what you'd like?"

"Yes."

Cléo took a drag of her cigarette and gazed out the window. Then she slipped the shirt over her head. Sitting there, like a native. She had small breasts, shallow curves like the palm of my hand, but with generous nipples. Dark, equatorial nipples. Hottentot tits. No one talked about tits then, especially in the Left. Objectification was taboo. But, with an equal duty to subversion, we all broke the rules in private. And seeing Cléo like that, sublimely stripped to the waist, I realized that I was crazy about her nipples, the way they showed through a sweater, the texture of them in my mouth, against my teeth, jujube antennae, sucked horizontal and stiff, magnified in the mind's eye. As she sat there, I could see them growing erect in the silence between us. I resisted an impulse to touch them, to embrace the familiar.

"*Alors*?" she said finally. "What are you thinking?"

"You. Your body. I don't think I've ever taken the time to look at you before."

"What do you see?"

"It's hard to say."

We kissed, slowly at first, with light, glancing tongues. I could taste the tobacco, metallic and foreign. She unbuttoned my shirt and lifted it off my shoulders. Then she unbuckled my belt, pulled it right out of the loops and draped it around my neck. There, your necklace, she said.

We laughed, and the facade of seduction dropped away. Falling onto each other with impatient, hardening mouths, we took off the rest of our clothes without a word.

CHARLEBOIS

I got accustomed to pure hallucination: I saw very clearly a mosque in place of a factory, a drumming school made by angels.

– Rimbaud, *Une saison d'enfer*

THERE WERE DAYS when I felt like a Brazilian boy at large, being ravished by the civilized world. Flirting on the fringes of some vast homosexual underground, slipping on satin shirts, feeling my hair curl down my neck, dancing, risking, fleeing from the terror of the gang. I had charm.

The day of the Charlebois concert, Cléo and I did acid. I wore my orange Algerian shirt and carried my orange rubber ball. We went to the Mountain late in the afternoon and played with the ball in the yellow light. Like everyone else in Montreal, I loved the Mountain, this ancient nub of a volcano, with the glow-in-the-dark cross marking the grave of an extinct fire. It seemed to be the whole *point* of the city, the town god. I found myself attracted to it, walking in its direction without knowing why. I would arrive routinely expecting magic, and rarely be disappointed. In the end, I developed quite a relationship with the Mountain, one that was as real as any other: it was my first volcano.

That afternoon with Cléo, I ran around feeling like a dog or a horse. I felt my muscles stretch and knuckle with flame. The sweat rose against the wind on my neck. When we were tired, we wandered over to the water fountain then up to the edge of the trees, where we watched a couple playing at romance. He was taking pictures of her. She was trying her best to be sexy. He was secretly seducing her. She didn't fool him. He didn't fool her. With Victorian intrigue they would lower each other's hurdles until the whole thing would be as easy and painless as taking a leak. The little clearing in the forest was their living room. That night there would be another little scene in the car. You could see long years of dull marriage spanning out in front of them. We crouched behind a log and watched them with contempt, as if we were nymphs and they were in our park.

We ran from the forest to the street and hopped a cab, out of the ripe afternoon and off to Place des Arts. So roomy! Such a wide ramp. Hundreds of people in clothes clinking against each other, each with a sharp eye for a better body, a flash of brown skin, a summer crotch, a gloss of hair seen from behind, inches away. So much self-conscious leisure. All heading down the ramp into this vast crimson shell, a plush mouth of mirrored teeth.

There was a tension in the crowd as it sized itself up. A shifting of thighs. People daring to look miles into the eyes of strangers. Hundreds of faces rustling about, rushing with blood. Our seats were at the center, near the front. I turned around and gazed up with disbelief at the bodies sweeping up to the ceiling. There was the excitement of a mob around a bonfire. You could smell the people—not the odor of tired feet and damp skin, but a dry scent of burning magnesium, an erotic friction rising and falling through the crowd in magnetic waves.

Their voices combined in the roar that precedes smoke, a low carnivorous sound. A shiver of excitement went down my back, a warm current rolling into a haystack. I turned to Cléo and said, "The crowd is burning. I mean *literally* burning, like there's a short circuit or something." I wondered if there really was a fire. I could smell smoke. Then I heard the instruments. Guitars were being sharpened behind the curtain, as if all the energy of the crowd were being wired to a single filament.

The curtain rose. The stage was in smoke. It was like a chamber of hell. At center stage, surrounded by a semicircle of Olympic torches, stood Charlebois, looking for all the world like a tamed leopard. Svelt, brazen and burlesque: a semi-naked savage looking at the boys and knowing what they like, his skin reflecting flames. A Latin with a lascivious smile and hair curled into a Fellini crown.

"*Je suis un troubadour perdu . . .*

. . . venu d'un autre moyen âge"

—I'm all that's left of what you knew—

"*J'ai voyagé comme j'ai vécu*

au coeur de l'alchimie des sages . . . "

Alchemy and voodoo. Alchemy and voodoo. On with the cult of the volcano!

When the curtain rose to reveal fire and smoke, I felt like a magician. For a split second my imagination overflowed with the possibility that I had some fantastic power and that the evening would be a spectacle of miracles, a magic show in which I was a vital accessory. A sorcerer's apprentice. I was in league with whatever was going to make it burn, or make people believe in things they never thought possible. We are in a strange town after dark, and there are movements behind the walls. Beyond the parapet, after a cold expanse of night air, there is still a blue glow where the sun used to be.

Charlebois turned from a soft rolling queen with gently weaving thighs and rounded shoulders and a blond acoustic guitar—he turned with a snapping fist into a rocker, fighting back tears with whips. With each of those transitions from female to male, I felt complicity—and guilt for those moments when I laughed secretly at his nakedness. The moment I betrayed him in my mind, the whip snapped, and I felt the lash of the electric guitar. The interaction had as much consequence as if our eyes, hands and tongues were locked in private passion. But not really private. We were dancing on a rock with our souls exposed to the universe. A black slate shelf brushing through space, watched by galaxies.

This time it wasn't a question of workers or bombs. There was nothing to fear. In art, as in smoke, all movements are permitted; the most selfish deliriums are legal. I felt utter affinity for this creature onstage. He was a cartoon rock star, the frog prince who served as Quebec's Elvis, Dylan, Jagger, Liberace and Apollinaire. He entertained delusions of abolishing gravity and winter. He sang of Dolores riding bare-naked in his Tornado; of stoned Latin *pistoleros* losing their bearings in the revolution; of Lindbergh, Gene Autry, Fu Manchu and *les cosmonautes*; of the pan-American dream in three-part harmony, *trois Amériques en unisson*; of his desire to be buried in a black piano.

His opening smile to the audience was a carnal invitation. Here we are, it said, welcome to my den of flames. I am a simple phoenix burning for your pleasure. Once I was unconscious, molten. Now I'm wearing the magician's manacles, the sexual vest of the court. I have become gaseous and cynical in my age, and my skin is stroked to a leather polish. I can make it rise and shine with the innocence of a boy remembering his mother's breast. I know a lot more than you think, more than I let on—otherwise it wouldn't work.

Although he was the sorcerer and I the apprentice, from the beginning I felt that I had some superiority over him. As if he were the genie who came and went only because I rubbed the lamp. During that first instant I was certain that I had lit those fires on the stage. I felt a surge of empathy for this *troubadour perdu*, for although he had free reign in the alchemist's kitchen, he was still a captive. Loved for his body and his voice, but a eunuch just the same.

During intermission, I pranced around the lobby carpets in my orange Algerian shirt, bouncing my orange rubber ball and feeling like a psychedelic lulu at a Sunday school picnic. The lobby was vast, with a great curving staircase rippling the carpet up to the balcony. Taking in the social breeze, I felt naked and brown under my clothes. I spotted someone I knew, Mike, a reporter from the newspaper. He was short and roundish with a face full of apostrophes, a comedian with a heavily creased forehead and a nervous laugh. He had bulging eyes. His whole face looked like it was holding back a brain as ripe as a cyst.

I noticed Mike and his girlfriend below in the lobby as I came down the stairs. For a while I stood just above their heads, watching them in secret. Then, after much premeditation, I let the rubber ball drop and bounce right between them. Mike looked up and I ran down and there were squeals of laughter and slaps on the back and one-liners spluttering out of Mike's mouth, which worked on the same ballast principle as his eyes—always brimming with incredulous glee. The way he looked at me, I could have been the *Kama Sutra* incarnate. I knew I had the arrogance, beauty and innocence of someone who was "coming out." I knew that what he saw was a far cry from the leather-jacketed marxomachine he knew from the office.

God knows what Mike and I talked about. I think he asked me the usual harmless question, "So, what are you doing?" Which I fielded on five million different levels before getting around to the one he was interested in. When you're not doing anything but throwing all your energy into the pleasure of your own emancipation, the question "What are you doing?" is like a pile of leaves.

By the time I got back into the theater I felt quite in command, slightly saner, and certainly at home. I didn't feel the same sense of anticipation among the audience. Their electricity had softened and mellowed. I sat there in my orange shirt with my orange ball, basking in the memory of my own event. Again the lights went down and the curtain went up. I couldn't believe my eyes. Projected on the backdrop of the stage, round and fat like the setting sun, was a gigantic *orange ball.* This was a bit much, even for me.

We walked out of the Charlebois concert into a thunderstorm. The skies were alive with forked lightning, and the tarmac surrounding Place des Arts was eel black and kicking up rain. I ran and danced on the roof of the world, lighting up the heavens with my toes. Electricity surged through my body, sparking in response to a psychic keyboard. There was nothing between me and the weather. It was that simple. My nerve endings were barking away at that big mother storm like a dog in heat. And as I recharged my cells, I felt a delicious mischief. The storm was a siren announcing my liberation, my ascension from earth to air. I didn't know then that the air would go dark and dry, or that from space the earth would never stop growing smaller. All that mattered was the thrill of transfusion.

The concert began and ended with fire. Charlebois: char, *cher, chair brûlée*, charred flesh, Charybdis. I felt the flick of his tail across my lips: a phosphorous embrace, Satan's *au revoir*. I loved him and burned him in a single breath. I swam back into wet-eyed childhood dreams, and woke up years beyond my age. As we danced on the tarmac, I didn't realize that it would never be the same, the shooting star that had charged me with its fire had been already eclipsed. Another god had come down to earth and died.

Cléo enjoyed the storm more than the show. When she told me the concert had left her cold, it was like having the magic carpet pulled out from under me. Without a corroborating witness, magic is quickly downgraded to mirage. I couldn't fathom her reaction. Cléo was as seduced by the idea of delirium as I was. She was the one who treated the writings of the French surrealists as gospel. She had an artist's appreciation for my more original tangents, and she encouraged me, up to a point. She said my problem was that I just didn't know where to stop, and she absolutely refused to play *maman*—even when I explained how I could cross busy streets without looking (by thinking of the color orange). I think she was a little jealous.

But she was curious to see how it would all turn out. And when I showed her the plane tickets, she was more than willing to go along for the ride.

We bought unlined notebooks and black drafting pens. She packed the acid, a blotter sheet of two hits each, which she slipped between the pages of Breton's *Surrealist Manifestos.*

SCILLA

CLÉO and the madman went to Italy, the southern part. There I was a wizard unborn, at one with the crescents and scythes that rule that part of the world. A Japanese photographer took pictures as I mixed candle wax and chemicals on the parapet overlooking the beach of the sirens.

I was an artist who built sand castles at full tide, insanely committed to the architecture of mirage. What rendered the dream real was the risk that something I considered marvelous would be rejected by others as noise.

There was no danger of eruption at Scilla, unlike the neighboring island of Stromboli. But there was something in the air. Soft, compelling and all too harmonious. Insidious as a dog whistle guaranteed to produce a dog. Sinuous insinuation: scales, coils, limestone shells curling into choral reefs, the siren shores. *Scilla!* You can hear snakeskin shuffle in the word itself.

Scilla is a village dominated by a rock rising several hundred feet out of *il mare violetto*, the sea that is cradled between the north edge of Sicily and the coast of Calabria. The Aeolian islands lie just under the horizon. That's where they keep the time machines stabled. According to the *Odyssey*, Scilla was home to the six-headed monster, across from the bottomless whirlpool called Charybdis. The waters are famous for their currents.

The Straits of Messina, which separate Sicily from the tip of the Italian boot, form a key intersection in a tectonic jigsaw. The town of Messina was swamped by a tidal wave at the turn of the century, and from Scilla's promontory, which is just up the coast, you can look across to Sicily and see a haze of smoke coming off the slopes of Etna—not just exhaust from the crater, but shrubbery burning on the mountain's back.

Scilla is quiet except for the slow carnivorous suck of the geraniums, which come in violet through cracks in the rock. A castle grows out of the rock, a twelfth-century castle with banked Turkish walls. Its stone walls slope out of the stubble cliff like a glans through foreskin, and from the labyrinth of cracks in the ancient stone creeps a fanatical vegetation. The ferns and flowers milk a dark force that seeps from the castle's buried guts, a shimmering black compost. The castle has secret chambers sunk far down into the rock, catacombs that were boarded up long ago, and are now said to be teeming with rats. These are some of the things we learned the longer we stayed in Scilla. There are no hotels in Scilla. We had to stay in the castle.

It's hard to know where the castle leaves off and the rock begins, impossible to imagine one without the other. The castle and the rock twist up from a maze of houses and churches. The rock sticks out into the sea like a carbuncle on the coastline, a peninsula dividing the village in two: on one side the beach, with its string of cafés and shops, and on the other the fishing port, where the houses go right down to the sea and have boats attached like parked cars.

To enter the castle you can climb any number of narrow paths to a road that hairpins up the spine of the rock. From the road, you walk up a cobbled ramp, bordered by thick stone walls. That in turn leads to a massive door, which is often locked. There are two bells on the wall, one for the youth hostel and one for the Navy, the two tenants of the castle. You ring the bell, and high up a head pokes through a hole in the stone and they send someone down to meet you. Beyond the door a stone walkway angles up above the town and the sea, overlooking a jetty where a big schooner is moored.

To get a bed in the hostel, you deal with Papa John, an old man with white hair, black-rimmed glasses, chewing gum hanging around his mouth. He wears black suit trousers and a white shirt with a black tie. He looks like a minor mafioso, and appears to be either senile or exceptionally crafty. He is always suggesting petty transactions of every sort to all comers. "Do you have any dollars?" But he seems more intrigued by the negotiation than by the sale. Above his desk in the castle lobby, where he greets travelers in the evening, are two signs. The first: TWO GIRLS WANTED IN SCILLA. The sign is never taken down and it seems to have always been there. Two girls are always wanted in Scilla. We had fantasies of sadistic priests and gangsters disposing of girls deep in the catacombs. We were sure something was going on down there. There is a tombstone on the castle floor engraved with a skull and crossbones.

Then there was the other sign: DON'T THROW STONES INTO THE SEA. I was never sure why stones were not to be thrown into the sea, whether it was dangerous for the fishermen, or the fish, or whether there was simply a shortage of stones. I wondered if it was philosophical—that throwing stones into the sea is stupid and pointless, and the sea doesn't like it. The last thing you want in a place like this is to get on the wrong side of the sea.

Scilla is the place where the secrets are stored, the scrotal rock. From there we went out to the Aeolian islands where sand floats, where men in wheelchairs smoke cigars and run porno caves deep in the trap-doored beachclubs, bomb shelters from the last war. Scilla was our stepping stone to the sea caves, the pumice coves, the black beaches, the clitoral boulder and the blue-eyed swordfish. In Scilla I discovered the semi-automatic spell of poetry, the spell that fans the flames as the ink dries, the incantation that brought the phoenix into my heart.

In Scilla, my eccentricity went unnoticed. It blended with the landscape, with the sing-song flux of the language, with the whispered messages that I detected on the flange of every indecipherable conversation: here gypsies ride up and down in trains controlling prices in their sleep; our stairways curve down to the sea and the land flows with congealed lava. From the first day, when the train pulled into the small station above the village and the welcoming voices of strangers beckoned like sirens, we felt the prickly warmth of being watched. A man in a bathing suit gave us a ride into the village. Step into my car, I'll take you, I was born here. Tearing down the mountain roads, he asked us if we had seen *Last Tango in Paris.* He found the English word for butter and ravished us with his eyes and his laughter while the car found its own way around the corners.

Cléo and I would sit in the beachfront café writing and drawing in our notebooks. We played two songs over and over on the jukebox: "Piccolo e Fragile," a pop ballad by an Italian girl, and "Rubber Bullets," by 10cc. One day a man came up and spoke into my ear in hushed, confidential tones: "I have seen your work. You are an artist. You will be like the others. Many great artists come to Scilla. They visit. Then they come back. They always come back."

One morning, I stood on the parapet overlooking the

sea and shaved off my beard, with brush and blade, re-enacting the scene in the opening chapter of Joyce's *Ulysses.* I held the bowl of lather up to the sky, a secular offering to the sun and the barking clouds, and pronounced incantations to the wind. Cléo held the mirror for me, placing it in front of her face, like a mask. My beard was a month old (shaving, like typing, was one of those habits that I had abandoned in favor of flow). As I drew the razor down my chin, I could feel clouds fall away, until my skin felt like the unfiltered blue sky of lost childhood. When I had finished, Cléo took the mirror from her eyes and gave a shriek of birthday glee, as if she had been given a fresh lover, as clean and sane as an untyped page. She stroked my face with both hands. Soft, like a baby's. I took the brush and painted a stripe of lather across her cheek, then the other cheek, her forehead and chin. Working more lather into the brush, I painted her whole face, finding the grain of her beauty in the brushstrokes, until she, too, looked like a stranger.

At the hostel, Papa John's men shut down the world for the night with flashlights. After curfew they'd sit there like gargoyles in the lamplight, with all the secrets of the castle flooding into their gothic cheekbones. I discovered that there is a curse on the castle. The secrets are safe because anyone who sees them appears to the outside world like a raving lunatic babbling the same alien code over and over again. The doctors shake their heads, and the peg-legged sailor's eyes go arching like umbrellas at the mere mention of *the map*.

I kept notes. Writing became my most powerful gesture, my ultimate revenge. My poetry made me invincible. I wrote nothing but what I saw, although to read it now, there is only the dried residue of hallucination, like the skin of a tropical fish whose colors go gray in the deadening air.

You must never stop believing in these hieroglyphics. I keep telling myself that. But as I sit here filing down the truth, a voice whispers in my ear: "Concrete facts. We want concrete facts." So you blubber out the bare essentials: that there is a garden and a wall.

One night in Scilla while she slept, I crept out of the castle at midnight, leaving the massive oak door ajar so I could re-enter, and went down to the nightclub by the beach. The scent of fratricide was in the air, carried in the black curls of beautiful women. I hung around with the regular patrons, who knew the barman. He broke up a fight between two young Calabrian men while the women watched with flared nostrils. It was the latest in an escalating series of fights that was bound to end in bloodshed. But that night the sides were calmed by the time the bar closed. A group of us went down to the beach and stripped off our clothes in the night air. I didn't know these people, but I could tell they were young jet-set gypsies, laughing and drunk. I stayed with them, silent as a boy, and they asked my name.

"Tango," I said after a pause.

"That's all?" asked a tall blond woman with crescent earrings.

"That's all. What's yours?"

"Treiza."

"Really?"

"Yes."

I dove into the black water and swam out into the waves, ducking under the surface like a porpoise to silence the laughter from the shore. As I came up for air I could feel moonlight slide down my back and over my ass.

"Tango, beware of the *pesce spada*! He will eat you."

I couldn't care about the voices from the shore. I was swimming in my own mystery. I imagined the *pesce spada*, the swordfish, as a soulmate in a sea compressed by the night into a radioactive world of secret communications spanning infinite space. Although my hair was turning silver at the age of twenty-five, I was a boy, a perfect child. Underwater, nothing mattered, not Treiza, not my androgynous sister sleeping inside the castle, not even the scheming hooded priests bent over their racks in the catacombs.

I emerged from the water. The moonlight rolled beads of mercury over my skin, now hard and tight from the breeze. The others jumped in and splashed around. They did not understand the sea, I thought. They had no respect. Later we built a small fire and warmed ourselves until we could throw on our clothes and rejoin the world of conversation and information.

Then Treiza and her friends left and I was alone again, free to wander the night. With my harmonica, I scared off evil spirits and sought out those that would bring me the song of the swordfish.

I was obsessed with fish. Fish that swim and dance to the disco of lines and nets. Fish frothing from my mind's eye, schools of synchronized arrows making sense of the flood, a cloud of compass points—fish nourishing my wish to locate the tail end of madness.

The fish-wish was *pesce spada*, symbol of my sex: now swimming at night through the bleak luster of the sea, now shrieking as a harpoon blade flies out of the dawn and into his polished skin, now sun-dry and dead in the back of a flatbed truck on the cobblestones of the village square, now being sliced into four-leaf-clover steaks, fresh and white and bloody, while women in black scramble for the choice cuts. *Pesce spada* gazing proud and silent through a giant blue-jelly eye, dry outside like cellophane but filled with the wetness of the sea, the retina swimming with memory, as alive as the stones and the wind, the African wind that sweeps up from the south like a pirate and steals sand into the sky.

I imagined eels and crabs and micro-fish shining with God's spasmodic light in the depths, singing the song of insects, a song forever caving in on itself, sucking the dance of creation into spirals of complicity, celebrating life with the ecstatic knowledge that it will end. The strongest repressed desire of any organism is to disappear. Every cell burns with the same question that keeps the rest of us awake. The less complicated creatures may lack philosophy, but they share with us the twin delusions of birth and death, the first mirage of consciousness: time, the bit of string that we leave behind so we can find our way back to the mouth of the cave.

In the morning I came across a fisherman repairing his nets on the beach, asked him if he had seen a cigarette package that I had left there the night before. It was stuffed with fragments of my dreams, including a peach skin imprinted with fossils I found embedded in a wall. He hadn't seen it. So, with a profound sense of loss, I decided I should abandon my ambition to be an artist and become a fisherman instead. Later on, having resigned myself to the loss—which at the time seemed tantamount to losing the entire manuscript of a novel in a fire—I found the cigarette pack in a garbage bin. Once again the world was without fault.

As I left the beach to walk up to the castle, the fisherman threw me a fish, just a few inches long, but a fish. I was elated. Then, climbing the stone stairways of the village, I met a beautiful boy who was making a bow and arrow. He said it was to catch fish.

"*Pesce spada?*" I asked.

"No, *piccolo,*" he said, indicating a small fish between his fingers. I showed him my fish and he laughed. My delusions, spawning more delusions, leaped up the dovetailed stream of coincidence. In the boy I saw myself as Ulysses stringing his bow, and thought about the symbolism of the arrow, the pun between *pesce* and *péché,* fish and sin, between *pêche* and *pêche,* peach and fishing, and between *flèche,* arrow, and *flesh.* It was going to be a busy, busy morning.

In the castle I arranged all the artifacts of my nighttime excursion: sticks, stones, papers, fruit and groceries, and this fish, *my fish.* In the hostel's kitchen, I combined them all into a mandala-like centerpiece for breakfast, a first supper for all humanity. One of the two girls who worked in the hostel (two girls wanted in Scilla) came in, looked at my little arrangement and froze in disbelief. I smiled with innocence and joy and explained it was a centerpiece for her breakfast table. She screamed and sent my artwork flying across the floor. I was furious and told her that she was an idiot, a sick victim of superstition.

I ended up weeping down by the castle gate. Helpless, insane and defeated. Another morning of anger and compromise had killed a night of dreams.

Can it be that nothing really happened? Of course, I acquired nothing tangible in those midnight reveries. I simply *went out,* out into the eyes of fish, into the stones of Scilla, into shadows dancing on moonlit waves, into a peach skin that I pressed against a wall and stuffed into a cigarette package for posterity.

But there was an absolute logic to my actions, for I lived in a perfect and endless code of symbols. Possession of mind was my obsession, mind possessing mind. I felt Scilla's transparent, skeletal depths run through my cells like coral sand. A single glance in the right direction, and I could raise seismic tremors. I worshiped space.

LIPARI

WE LEFT SCILLA and crossed the Straits of Messina on a boat, where I deciphered messages of apocalyptic destruction from the coded vibrations of the engine. That evening we walked through the streets of Messina, along hillsides where the garbage and the flowers were all mixed up, just like in the Leonard Cohen song. We spent the night in a *pensione* and could finally fuck like adults without fear of being discovered.

At the hostel in Scilla, Cléo and I had slept in separate dorms. It was hard to find places for sex. One night we agreed to rendezvous after curfew in the garden. We snuck out of our bunks and met at the castle parapet. Whispering, we crawled through an arch in the thick wall and made love on a cold slab of medieval stone. There wasn't much room. We sat side by side on the ledge necking, then peeled off our jeans. I lifted her onto me. We had quick, purposeful sex, jack-knifed together, with her legs wrapped around my back and me hanging onto her waist as she cantilevered over the edge. "Don't let go," she said, only half joking.

Another night while walking the road that circled the shore at the base of the cliff, we found a small hideaway in the rock. It seemed dark enough. We began to make out. I slipped a hand under her shirt, over the small scallop breasts (she never wore a bra). I felt the racing hardness of a nipple crease my palm. She hurried with my belt and zipper. My fingers found the wetness under her skirt, and she had my cock in her hand, when suddenly we were stopped cold by a blaze of headlights. Hoots of derision from a gang of men. We looked around in a panic and saw that our little niche, now brightly lit, was some sort of Catholic shrine.

One afternoon in Scilla we made love while standing in the sea, trying to get a purchase in the lobbing sway of the water. Cléo couldn't stop laughing. She would become a sea nymph in the water. Her eyes turned a brilliant, mischievous green against the waves. She liked making love in secret, in public. On the plane coming over, while most of the passengers slept, she snuck her head under my blanket and took me in her mouth. I kept my eyes closed, pretending I was dreaming while trying to convince myself I wasn't.

By the time we reached Messina, I was without glasses. I had broken them in Scilla, hurled them onto the cobblestone ramp leading up to the castle, which made me feel immense relief, like the time I had my watch stolen in the Caribbean. I'm very near-sighted, and without glasses anything more that two feet in front of me melts into an impressionist blur. I couldn't recognize faces. I couldn't read price tags. But I became more attuned to sounds, to the calliope rhythms of the Italian language, and with the dissolution of edges—of focus. Facts and details became even more irrelevant than before. I would miss nothing important; I had a good excuse. The arbitrary line dividing past and future became a creamy blur.

But that night in Messina, the ancient crossroads between Italy and Sicily, I felt a shudder of realism as I noticed that we had passed the halfway point in our trip. Over rough red wine in an empty café, Cléo and I talked about our plans. She was never one to discuss "the relationship," except in the most absolute terms. Talk of marriage was taboo. We were together by accident, for the pursuit of passion, like two friendly nations under one sail, for as long as the wind would carry us.

"You ever wonder what it would be like to just keep going?" she said.

"Go where?"

"Wherever we end up."

"But we've got an excursion fare."

Even with my mind in tatters, I maintained a healthy respect for airplane tickets.

"We could always sell the tickets," she said.

"But where would we go?"

She shrugged. "We could look for Bertolucci."

That was a fantasy of hers. Being discovered by Bertolucci.

"What do we do when the money runs out?"

"We could be gypsies." She laughed. I always felt like her father in these scenes, even though I was supposed to be the crazy one.

"What about the apartment?"

"We could arrange something. Anyway, it was just an idea."

"Well, I like the idea," I said. "It's a great idea. Maybe I could become a diver."

Her eyes had gone cold.

"You're probably right," she said.

Silence. A leather boy on a motorcycle pulled up. He looked at us, shared a joke with the barman, then roared off into the night.

"It doesn't really matter what we decide," she said. "And I don't care where we end up. But I've always thought we should go as far as we can. Then when we reach the end, we should know it's the end. *Point final.*"

"Like *Last Tango.*"

"Like *Last Tango.*"

"What will happen once we go back?" I asked. "Do you think we'll break up?"

"We could."

From Messina, we set off for the Aeolian archipelago, an arc of seven volcanic islands cradled between Italy's Calabrian coast and the northeastern edge of Sicily. They are home to Aeolus, the Greek god who gave Ulysses a pigskin bag of winds that blew him on a roller-coaster ride to hell and back, by way of Scilla and Charybdis. The seabed around the islands, a sort of Tyrrhenian triangle, is littered with ancient wrecks. The waters are known for their strange winds and currents, and so is the earth beneath them.

We had time for two islands. Lipari is the largest in the chain: a volcanic boneyard with rock formations of twisted black obsidian and floating beaches of white pumice. The other was Stromboli, an active volcano ringed by black sand: the Lighthouse of the Mediterranean.

Scilla, Lipari, Stromboli. The words have become incantations to me. They were just places then, destinations of the moment. But now, in the mythology that I've constructed to triangulate my past, they loom like seasonal coordinates of the soul—Scilla, the rock-garden Purgatory, towering like an Escher maze of stairways and gates; Lipari, the uncontainable Paradise where memory floats suspended like dust in sunlight; and Stromboli, the live crater that leads, like a cartoon with glaring signposts, to the Inferno.

Lipari's most recent colonists are Mafia exiles. We would

sense their presence in ambiguous glances and in the lanes that ended in walled compounds. After disembarking from the ferry, we sipped cappuccino and wrote postcards in the port, then set out to find a floating beach that travelers had told us about. We hitched a ride up the coast highway. On the inland side of the road, there were mountains of what looked like salt—pumice dust from the mines. The car let us off. We looked for a way down, then found a footpath that faded into nothing. Far below, we could see a couple of white crescent beaches, joined by a small point. We made our way down a rugged hillside, past wild geraniums and thistles growing through cracks in the rock. It was steep. Thorns scratched our tans and tore at Cléo's long cotton skirt.

By the time we reached the cove, our bodies were stinging with sweat. We took off our shoes and tested the pumice sand. It was a porous white powder, more like cocaine than quartz. Near the shore, clouds of it hung suspended in the waves, turning the water creamy turquoise. We were alone. We walked over to the rocks and shed our clothes. Cléo got the acid out of her bag, two tiny blotter squares with strawberries printed on them.

Naked under a clear sky, we swam and waited for the drug to come into focus. In the shallows the sand billowed up, enveloping our bodies like whipped egg white.

We lay down together in the ebb of the waves. Cléo lay on her back, letting the water slide up her legs and lap her cunt, her African bush, which was surprisingly thick and voluptuous for her boyish frame. Lying on my side, I watched a wave rush between her thighs, flashing over the smooth rock of her belly, leaving beads of sunlight stranded in pubic hair. A sea cave bearded with moss. I rinsed the sand from my fingers and explored her slippery warmth, the soft-bladed crease. My cock darkened between us. With the other hand, I rolled grains of white pumice over her skin, dusting her breasts, the Egyptian nipples rising straight and hard to the touch.

Cleo gazed down at her body, as mesmerized by it as I was.

Magnified by the acid, every caress became encyclopedic. There was more detail than we knew what to do with—textures that came off in our hands like gold dust, contour lines of friction and perfume. Sex was another thing altogether. It gathered somewhere inside, like weather. The act itself seemed almost inconceivable.

I knelt between her legs and kissed her there, playfully at first, trying to get over the impression that I was face to face with a sea anemone. I explored with my tongue, looking for the familiar places, the almond edges.

"That feels strange," she said.

I looked up. "Is it too much?"

"I'm not sure. You're very far away."

I moved back to her side. We began to kiss each other ever so slowly on the lips, like shy teenagers in love with the newness of it all. For the longest time, we just gazed at each other, inches away, smiling uncontrollably and trying to find words for the obvious.

"I wish you could see your eyes."

"I wish you could see yours."

Hers were green and rayed with amber. They went on forever.

I remember discovering something about the speed of light. That it wasn't all that fast. Sifting through a fingerprint file of colors that could be detected in her skin. Her shining clit. The taste of her, salty wet then dried to an electric finish by the sun. Her fascination with my cock, which had a life of its own, independent from both of us, and which she photographed obsessively, like a rare creature that she had cornered in the wild. The sperm that dreamed its way back to the sea. An orgasm, cracking like a peach pit. But I don't think either of us remember what happened, or how we made love, or how it ended, aside from the knowledge that we would never share a more perfect moment. Even now, when we meet for a civilized drink every six months or so, she sometimes talks of Lipari in discreet, reverent tones, as if it were a sacred relic, a piece of paradise that no amount of separation can diminish.

That afternoon was when I first sensed it was going to unravel. Trying to recall that day is like prying a memory out of infancy. But a few things stand out. The clitoral boulder: a large pink boulder with a sea-washed cleft that had the distinct contours of a clitoris. Cléo discovered it and showed it to me. It was hers; I could only admire it.

Later, a sailor man in a bumblebee shirt cruised by in a little dingy, watching. Reminding us we were not alone.

At the end of the day, a cold wind came up. A lone black bird cut low across the sky, wheeling away from the island, away from the weakening sun, a knife's shadow passing through my heart.

We didn't climb back up to the road through the thorns. Farther down the shore, we found a path that zigzagged up the cliff past tiny houses, broom-swept caves of ceramic tile etched into the hillside. We trespassed around corners, walking through the electric shock of a black cat jumping from a wall, and around the malevolent stare of a man corruptly poised between a wheelchair and gold cigarette holder. By the time we reached the road, the air was nettled with conspiracy.

That night, as the acid wore off, she drew while I wrote:

"Babies cry above the music voices come up from the beach bend buzz coalesce convalesce the sand between your thighs how they swell out hairless inside like a girl what did you think of the man in the café that german boy so nice these italians as if they didn't wear any underwear do you think really but it's such a long walk back perhaps no I wish there was a bed cheap somewhere what's the sky doing caving in at this time of day the moon is awfully help the birds have seen us the old man in the boat stripes the jolly boat his umbrella he looked as if he owned our bodies have secret cameras where would they put us on the beach hollow false bottom silent fins not solid at all when you think about it breath lost between these atoms crying like your hair in this light why are you cold take mine looking forward to dinner why can't it be like this all the time you'll never forget will you not even when we're old no matter what happens when we're dead look at that bird so black slow wings out but how strange as if yes really strange watching us strange eyes in the cliff strange spirit or machine strange bat with fur under his orange fur under his arms this fine dust spun dry waves pumice beads kneading in out among your ovaries why do they look at us so strange as if we were watch that man in the car and how he receives his instructions from the fire on the mountain."

STROMBOLI

IN SOUTHERN ITALY, between the magnetic fields of the Mafia and the harmonic beach of the sirens, I found a motherlode of evidence to enrich my paranoia. After a while, I think I began to develop an immunity. By the time we got to Stromboli, delusions had become so commonplace, so available, that I was reconsidering the merits of sanity, that convenient and necessary fiction.

Some facts: Stromboli erupts every ten or twenty minutes and has been doing so quite consistently since the beginning of recorded history. Of the world's thousands of active volcanoes, it is one of just four that have such a regular breathing pattern. Its cone rises from the deep waters of the Tyrrhenian Sea. The summit is slightly more than half a mile above sea level, but another mile of the volcano lies under water. A fireberg.

The Aeolian arc circumscribes a navel in the dead center of the Mediterranean. It is the intersection where the

African and European plates of the earth's crust collide. Under the torsion, the Italian boot is being gradually pushed counterclockwise. The pressure finds release in lava flows at Etna, and builds up, like bad memories in a psychotic mind, under Vesuvius, a time bomb that will devastate Naples sooner or later. About halfway between Etna and Vesuvius lies Stromboli, the eye of the hurricane. The island's name comes from the Greek *strombos*, meaning circle. Everything about the place is circular, from the endless cycle of eruptions to the spiral winds that weave around its shores.

The island is not safe. Although the daily eruptions that percolate from the crater pose no immediate danger, there is always the threat of something bigger. There have been three major eruptions this century, the most recent in 1930, which blew 230 feet off Stromboli's summit, hoisted the entire island three feet out of the water, caused a tidal wave and killed eight people. Four died trying to escape by sea. One was swept away by boiling water.

Nineteen years later, Ingrid Bergman and Roberto Rossellini came to the island to make a movie, and make love. Their affair scandalized America. Bergman—a married woman, a mother, a blond icon of Hollywood virtue—was fucking a dark, balding Mediterranean filmmaker, who also happened to be married. The movie, about a Latvian girl who marries a crude Strombolian fisherman and follows him to his barren island of fire and ash, was forgettable, but the production was not. A crewmember died in Stromboli's toxic fumes. Isabella Rossellini's younger brother, Roberto, was conceived on its shores. And the shock waves of her mother's infidelity reached all the way to the U.S. Congress, where a senator denounced "the stupid film about a pregnant woman and a volcano," while speculating that Bergman might be the victim "of some kind of hypnotic influence."

He was referring no doubt to her swarthy foreign suitor. But it is more likely that the hypnotic influence belonged to the island itself. We spent just a day and a night there, and you could tell right away it was the kind of place where romances began or ended.

On the bow deck of the ferry, Cléo lay asleep in the sun, reclined on a coil of rope. Next to her: the nutbrown bodies of three local boys sprawled half-naked, like castaways cruising the Mediterranean, young pirates with smooth limbs and delinquent mouths. She could have been one of them.

Stromboli appeared on the horizon like a Japanese painting, a pyramid floating on a film of mist. As we got closer, the wind quickened and the water suddenly seemed deeper, more like the ocean. The pyramid's symmetry slowly gave way to austere contours: sheer black slopes and violent folds in the rock. A lacework of houses came into view along the shore. Then a gray flower of ash unfolded from the crater, in silence and slow motion.

The ferry anchored offshore. A rowboat took us to the

beach below the island's main village, located on the one strip of coast where the mountain's severe angles didn't plunge straight into the sea. Behind the village, cane-grass fields sloped uphill, faintly scored with the terrace lines of abandoned vineyards. Cubic houses, stark and white with Moorish corners and small windows, formed a chiaroscuro pattern against black rocks and black sand. The island had no cars.

The strangeness of the place was palpable. First as a sweet, narcotic scent, disturbing but not unpleasant. I never did find out what it was. Someone suggested oleander. I always associated it with the fine ash that falls continually from the crater, invisible in the air, but collecting over the course of a couple of hours as black filings on a white table.

From the boat, we walked up through the laneways that slant through the village. We were told we might find a room at the far end. There, perfectly good houses were interspersed with ruins, black shells of volcanic rock, the stucco crumbling away. We followed a powdery black path up through the cane grass and met a young woman coming the other way, carrying a wicker basket and singing "Somewhere Over the Rainbow."

She welcomed us as though she'd known we were coming. An English girl. Dark hair, deep tan, barefoot, a sarong knotted at the waist, breasts clearly shadowed under a white blouse. She worked for a landlord who owned a place up the path. It was a squat little stone hut that stood by itself in a field. She fiddled with the rusty padlock and showed us in. The room was tiny, nothing but a bed on a stone floor with wooden bedposts that seemed too big for it.

"Pretty basic, I'm afraid," said the girl. "How long do you plan to stay?"

"Two nights," said Cléo.

"But you just got here."

"We'd stay longer if we had more time," I offered, wondering why I felt we owed her an apology.

"We were in Lipari," said Cléo.

"Oh, Lip*ari*," repeated the girl, making the word sound terribly English.

"And now we're going back," I said.

"Back to Lipari."

"No, back home," said Cléo. "To Canada."

"Oh, you're going *back*. That's a shame."

We gave her the money. She gave us the key. We dumped our stuff in the room, went down to the beach with the last two bits of blotter and walked along the shore, away from the village. The utter peculiarity of the place began to sink in. We had the constant feeling of being watched.

Walking on Stromboli was like trespassing on the skin of a living creature. The earth felt hollow underfoot, more like a ceiling than a floor. All the rocks looked as though they had been put there, positioned just so. Their surface was rough and porous, unpolished by wind or water.

There was an existential clarity to each moment on the island. The volcano was like a clock with its own arbitrary yet indisputable sense of time. Walking along the path, I'd feel something tickling the back of my mind and I'd turn around to look up at the mountain. Then, right on cue, a fresh cloud of ash would mushroom from the summit. This would happen again and again. It punctuated the day. I couldn't hear the eruptions from the village, or even feel them. I don't know what made me look up. Cléo found the same thing happening to her.

Beyond the village, a long black-diamond beach stretched to a rocky point. We walked almost to the end, past some German girls playing nude in the waves, then took off our clothes. The sand was too hot for bare feet. We ran shrieking into the water. For the Mediterranean, it was cold, and the bottom shelved off quickly, turning the water a deep, violent blue. We didn't stay in. Feeling our bodies drying hard in the wind, we walked along the wet edge of the sand, to the point where the beach ended in a jumble of moon rocks.

That is where I sat and watched Cléo pound two stones together and tell me that she would be happy to be a stonemason, alone in the world for the rest of her life. There was no drama in the way she said it. It wasn't even personal. But when she looked at me, her eyes were as unyielding as the rock in her hands. For the first time on the trip, I felt hopelessly lonely.

Late in the afternoon we went back into the village and

up to the white-domed church that was the only notable landmark. We climbed past it, higher up the slope through the abandoned vineyards until we could look down on the village. In some places, if you stare long enough, hidden images emerge. I stared at a church dome, which floated like a Moroccan mirage, mandalas forming in the sea behind it. I asked Cléo if she could see it. She asked me not to disappear into my head.

As we walked back down, Cléo noticed shards of broken glass set in cement along the top of the stone wall around the church. Broken bottles, like shark's teeth. Cléo's paranoia was often a match for my own. She saw Nazi cults behind every locked gate, every private beach. But we both agreed that the wall was creepy. Why would they need to keep people out of a church? Later she referred to the wall as *la ligne de verre pointu.* She had a way of making things sound more sinister in French.

That night we ate swordfish at a restaurant run by Germans. (Stromboli seemed to be owned by Germans.) After dinner, we wandered through the dark laneways, using a flashlight to find our way, for there were no streetlights. Near the shore we came across a deserted outdoor dance floor, a terrace overlooking the ocean.

"It's closed," I said.

"Maybe it doesn't open till late."

"It's already late."

We climbed the steps onto the dance floor. I took her hand and swung her around to imaginary music. Just then, we heard the low whine of a generator starting up. Above our heads, strings of Christmas lights went on. Loud music, "Gimme Shelter," started up over the sound system. A man, who had suddenly materialized out of the dark, sat at a turntable under a red light in the corner. We began to dance, shyly at first, then taking up the whole floor. Posing and prancing for each other. The man playing the record watched us intently, like a voyeur.

As Cléo danced she seemed to be taunting me, or him. Her legs, spidery in black jeans, moved hard and quick across the floor. I followed, bisecting flamenco angles, eking sparks out of her curves. She threw off her jacket. Underneath, she wore a sheer blue Indian shirt. We had the dance floor to ourselves, but it felt more like a stage, with the two of us competing as soloists for attention, performing alone, for each other, under the volcano.

The music stopped. We turned to the man. He cued up another song. More Rolling Stones. "Sympathy for the Devil." We danced in and out of each other's sidelong glances, circling like boxers from our respective corners. Our hips grazed, and as her waist spun out of my hands, I felt a cool slice of skin under her shirt (her skin was always colder than mine). We whirled away at each other like that, shadow-dancing, while the man in the corner watched, until we were exhausted.

We went over and thanked the man profusely, as if he were some sort of magician.

"*Uno momento*," he said.

He scribbled something, handed it to us.

It was a bill for 10,000 lire.

"For the dancing," he said in Italian.

We looked at each other in disbelief.

I laughed. "Maybe you should pay us." But he wasn't smiling.

"Ten thousand lire."

We argued. He pretended not to speak English. Finally we gave him 5,000 lire and left while he shouted after us, threatening to call the police. We ran and ran, through the dark village and down to the sea.

We decided not to go back to the room but to spend the night on the beach. It got chilly. We huddled around a candle and watched the flame melt down then disappear into a driftwood log. There was no moon. Behind us the volcano could be seen only as a black triangle cut out of the stars. We talked about what we would do if the volcano erupted, whether it would be safer to flee by land or by sea. Cléo seemed thrilled by the possibility of apocalypse. I think she liked the idea of her world and the one around us ending neck and neck.

We sat looking out to sea, mesmerized by the lights of squid boats shifting on the waves. We felt a little let down by the volcano. We hadn't seen any fireworks.

"It doesn't do much," I said. "Maybe it's not what it's cracked up to be."

"Maybe it's a dud," she said.

At that moment there was a low rumble, and we turned

to see the crater send a long red flare into the night. We shrieked and shivered and held each other close, wondering what we'd do if the whole place went up with us on it.

The next day, I decided to climb to the crater. Cléo, who thought we were close enough as it was, stayed behind. We had a bit of an argument. It was our last day in the islands. Cléo said it was a stupid idea to climb a live volcano. She said she'd heard it was dangerous and people shouldn't go up without a guide. When I said I didn't want to bother with a guide, she told me to do whatever I liked and went back to reading her book.

Late in the afternoon, I set out alone to the end of the village and followed a brick footpath that zigzagged up through the cane grass. Soon it turned into a trail of gray ash, with dense yellow thickets on each side. Looking down, I could see the wind stirring spiral patterns on the sea. As I climbed, a dark cloud moved in from the northwest and circled the summit while the rest of the sky stayed blue. There were rumblings of thunder and a faint sweat of rain. Then the cloud left as quickly as it had come.

Two-thirds of the way up, the vegetation ended and the path grew steep. Hard ribs of cayenne rock protruded through a loose rubble of stones and pumice. The trail bordered a ridge that cleaved down on the right to a severe slope called the Sciara del Fuoco, the fire road—a black hypotenuse that cut straight from the summit to the sea, like a slide. It was smoking with fresh debris from the crater.

Near the top, the path went up a dune of powdery black sand that slipped away with each step, like an uphill beach. The landscape looked alpine, but everything that should have been white was black, as in a negative.

Behind me, I heard a voice calling. I turned to see a man coming briskly up the trail behind me. He introduced himself as Franz Kohler, the island's resident volcanologist, a German. As we continued the climb together, he was eager to explain himself. Franz said he used to work as an engineer in a Mercedes factory and drive racing cars. Now that his passion for internal combustion had shifted from cars to volcanoes, he always brought his old crash helmet with him on expeditions to the crater.

As a race driver, Franz had so many accidents that they called him Catastrophe Kohler. But he was never seriously hurt. He had his worst accident on a bicycle as a teenager. A tire blew as he was trying to overtake a truck, which rolled over his leg. "All the meat was pressured," he said, stopping to show me a nasty scar below his shorts.

The sun was setting by the time we reached the crater, a natural amphitheater carved out of the summit by the explosion of 1930. The inner walls sloped down to a smoldering pit of smaller, active craters. There was a smell of sulfur.

As Franz took off his pack, his helmet came loose. It bounced and skittered down to the bottom of the pit, rolling all the way to the lip of the farthest crater, the one at the edge of the Sciara del Fuoco. Explaining the helmet had great sentimental value, he scampered down after it. He was halfway across the pit when the eruption started.

It began with a dry ripping sound, which became a roar as a column of ash and glowing rocks surged into the air. The fountain climbed to about two hundred feet. Then, as it subsided, a shower of rocks clattered to the ground. Overhead, ash billowed into a mushroom cloud, a dark shape slowly distended by the wind. I found myself wanting to applaud.

I had expected Franz to run away from the eruption. But he just stood there watching. When it was over, he continued on to the edge of the crater and picked up the helmet. He lingered for a while before climbing back up to join me. Delighted to have it back, he showed me where the fall had cut a deep gouge in the cherry red plastic.

"If this is what happens when a light helmet falls a hundred metres and hits a rock," he grinned, "you can imagine what happens when a five kilo rock lands on your head from a height of a hundred metres."

In the descending twilight, we sat and watched the eruptions. Something happened about every ten minutes. The craters performed like a three-ring circus. One hurled up fountains of rock and ash. It was the main event, the one that made the mushroom clouds. Near the edge of the Sciara, where Franz had gone to fetch his helmet, another coughed up orange lava that coagulated in midair and fell back to the ground as rocks. Between them was a third feature consisting of two holes, like eyes in the ground, that burned with a low red fire. They made the seething sound of surf being sucked through a grotto. Every so often they roared with twin jets of blue flame.

The volcano had one more trick, a wild card. It involved no eruption, just an ear-splitting detonation beneath our feet, like an underground thunderclap.

"What the fuck was that?" I asked Franz.

"Gas. Gas in Stromboli's stomach."

The repertoire of effects added up to a persuasive personality. An intra-terrestrial intelligence. It was enough to make the agnostic in me propose unconditional surrender: Okay, I *believe.* You have my full attention. I'll do whatever you want.

Kohler turned to me with a wild look. "You want to go down and see the vent?"

It was like being asked by an older kid to go play on the railway trestle.

"Is it safe?"

"Yes, I think now it will be quite safe. Here, you can wear this."

He handed me his helmet. I put it on and followed him down to the main crater. Near the edge, we walked into a cloud of noxious fumes, and Franz told me to stop breathing as he led us around the rim to a spot outside the smoke. The crater was a black oval pit the size of a surburban basement. It was lined with glowing coals, a giant hibachi. Franz tried to point out the vent, the small mouth where the eruptions came from. I scanned the puzzle of smoldering debris but couldn't find it.

"Well, I'm satisfied," I said after a reasonable pause. "Let's get out of here."

"What? You do not want to stay for an eruption?"

"Not really."

"I think you will find it very interesting."

"It can't be *that* interesting."

"You will never know unless you see it."

We waited. Utter madness—standing at the gates of hell and waiting for them to fly open, with nothing but a crash helmet and the reassurance of a man called Catastrophe Kohler.

My eyes were still searching for the vent when it happened. With a shuddering explosion, a geyser of rock and ash shot up right in front of us. I jumped back from the heat of the blast, but Franz gripped me by the arm.

"Don't run away," he yelled. "Look up! It's beautiful!"

The column churned high above our heads, like a cartoon genie. For a moment, it stood suspended at its apogee, and then the rocks began to fall. Tracking their trajectory like a scared outfielder, I noted with relief that they were all raining down at a safe distance in front of us. Then there was a heavy thud behind us. And half a dozen more.

"Franz," I said, as we climbed out of the area, "I thought you said it was safe."

He looked at me as if I was quite mad.

"Nowhere is safe here. It is very, very dangerous."

We made our way back down the mountain in the dark, Franz leading the way. Our flashlights played over the path, illuminating the volcanic dust kicked up by our feet. A dreamlike momentum set in, a rhythm of skidding and sliding. Like Alice down the rabbit hole, we dropped through tunnels of bush and briar, past monstrous shapes that veered into the crooked light. Franz talked about an instinct that tells him when it's safe to go near the vent. He said that the Chinese used snakes to predict earthquakes, and that we probably still have a seismic sensor in our reptilian brain. I wondered if our dreams were descended from magma, if our unconscious evolved from an early warning system responding to storms in a subterranean sea . . . if magma is literally the stuff of dreams.

We emerged from the thickets, and the summit popped back into view behind us, the black triangle cut from the stars. I felt the chilling clarity of déjà vu, of having been there not just before, but forever. I took a last look up at the crater, expecting an answer, and it replied with a faint flare.

"You are lucky," said Franz before we went our separate ways. "Tonight we have nice eruptions."

In the room, Cléo was asleep. I took off my clothes and slid under the covers beside her. She stirred. Her body curled around my back, like a leaf. With my eyes closed, I could see my warmth ebb into the cool darkness of her skin. Wide awake, I lay there for a long time, hallucinating quicksand.

The next thing I remember, we were on a train, heading for Rome, in a private compartment with two gypsies and a priest. I was doing mad collages with cigarette wrappers, cutting them into triangles and constructing volcanoes on paper. Talismans without aesthetic or artistic value. But I considered them works of absolute magic. The gypsies and the priest watched in silence, trying to decide if I was an artist or a madman. Meanwhile, Cléo slept like a small boy, an orphan pirate in a den of thieves. No one was quite sure whom she was with, so everyone regarded her protectively, each treating the others as potential killers and rapists. They were not even certain of her sex, and I could tell they were bewitched by her androgyny. As the train rushed through the night, they kept their voices to whispers. But I could feel their thoughts.

It was some time later in Rome that I looked at the cigarette-pack-volcano collage and saw Cléo's brief sentence written at the top. I can't quote it verbatim, but it spoke of unsuspecting tourists being in the presence of a sinister force operating just behind the veil of paradise. She didn't say that; she would never say anything like that. She did, however, lump *la ligne de verre pointu* of Stromboli and the murder at Scilla into the same sentence.

There was a murder in Scilla on the last night we spent

there. One man knifed another in the bar down by the water. It was in the paper. We found out about it the next day in Reggio di Calabria while waiting for the train to Rome. At the station, a white-haired man with a slightly crazed look in his eyes came up to us and said he had noticed us in Scilla. He pointed to the story in the paper and told us in a whisper that the murder had been Mafia business. The police had called it a crime of passion. I wanted to believe it was both, and I felt a brief thrill of identification with the killer, or was it the victim? From this distance, I'm in no position to judge, and I'm past caring. I'm sane now.

CHARYBDIS

CLÉO LEFT ME for a guitar player in Toronto, a gentle narcissist with curly black hair and reptile green eyes. She said she had finally found a man just like her. She broke the news over spring rolls in a Vietnamese restaurant, said he was coming to stay for a few days at the apartment. I was open-minded, but there were limits. I said I wouldn't stand for it. She said that I had no choice, that she had her own life, her own room. She suggested that I go somewhere else for a few nights. Even in those days of sexual license, this all seemed a bit much. I decided to stay put. Late at night, as I lay in bed, I heard them creep in and have whispered sex in the room next door. I growled and tore the bedsheets with my teeth until they stopped. They found somewhere else to stay.

The next day I went back to the machine, the upright Underwood acoustic, ripped out a half-typed page of Italian memoir, and began pounding on the round black keys.

"As I write I am overtaken by events. The season of my madness has come around again, its first anniversary. I feel it lapping at my brain, the bloody month of March, kicking my crutches into the spring flood. This is no longer the stale aftermath, the flat trackless life of the fall and winter months, drifting in romantic memories of a brown-backed summer, naked with Cléo in Italy. I had that story safely stowed away like a sacred treasure, to be gently pried open years later with wisdom and sacramental caution. But my vantage point has disappeared under my feet. Cléo left me. I let it happen.

"There's no pretending this is a novel. It's a swirling cloud of splinters, flying in slow motion, forwards, backwards, frozen in suspension, spring forward, fall back, holy incest of the seasons. There is, however, an intended story. Its subject has slipped under the horizon, but I feel its spell pulling on the dark side of my mind. Behind the one-way mirror, seawaves of ultraviolet memory—*il mare violetto*—have me in their spell, like the sirens who inhabit the mirage. This magnetic sea is dry like a mirror, like fiction, like romance. You pay for truth with lies.

"*The stories lie ahead. The story is a liar. The lie heads the story. The story gives head.*

"All of this—suicide notes, manifestos, Canterbury tales—reflects nothing more than vertiginous desire. It is no more meaningful or poetic than a man going over the falls in a barrel. No matter why the man does it, no matter what he's trying to prove, who he's trying to be, what he's trying to say or sell or release or destroy, he's still just a man going over the falls in a barrel. And *what*, what else is there?"

"A fantasy: We were found with communism in our pockets, strung up naked against the blackboard. We escaped, caught the teacher, stripped off her gray suit and slowly dusted her breasts with blackboard brushes. You can still see the areolas, mauve and dark under the chalk.

"I shall not buff my teacher's breasts with blackboard brushes. I shall not buff my teacher's breasts with blackboard brushes. I shall not buff my teacher's breasts . . ."

"Getting back to the work at hand, there are two things to clear up before I can pry open the treasure chest, string the doubloons into fiction with characters and plot: a situation and a character beyond myself. The situation is suicide. The character is Charybdis (formerly Cléo), who enters the stage precisely because she has left. Charybdis, whose phantom must now be dealt with, whose betrayal galvanizes my story into 'true' romance—a lie. Charybdis, whose laugh is more dangerous than anything she owns, including her orgasm, which is at best a lament and a surrender. But her laugh, the cackle of a young svelt witch, sends waves flying, wires burning, mocks all that is monastic or masonic."

"Charybdis, I lost the will in my mind to stay alive, found a petty scratch with a mirror and a razor blade. The cat is screaming for attention and the trees are growing like a farm in a desperate wind. I hang on to the carriage lever of the typewriter like a helm."

"Charybdis, I miss the hard flick of your switchblade ass. My breast is warm and wide in my palm, and my nipple asks why you left the bed. The lament continues in white robes and desert dust, and in long silent bouts over Arabian coffee. You say you'd be happy all alone with objects, an astronomer lost in space. You say you don't need people. So why do you always have one running, one in full bud, one dying on the branch and one conspiring to meet you in the whaling rooms of your imagination?

"A certain sadness, a certain fond regret, some hysteria, and at times the desire to crush you like a bug. I killed a big fat bug in the sunny concrete of the Université de Montréal. A queen wasp with a long hard belly. She crawled all the way up my leg, and I could feel an intimate communication developing between us as I studied her and she slowed down. I'd had this kind of experience with mosquitoes in Italy, intimate and suspenseful affairs that would go on until one side or the other broke the trust. With the mosquitoes, love would eventually give way to fear, and then they would sting, as if they sensed the change of climate on my skin. My betrayal always came first. Likewise with the wasp. I killed it hard. It went flying off onto the step beside me and lay on its back, squirming. I crushed it with my foot. This has nothing to do with you. I would kill you with a knife."

"Charybdis, you must must must understand that I loved you and still do and come to the typewriter not out of some arithmetic desire to bridge the gap and communicate, but to break the slow agony of the late-afternoon sun. That thick yellow sun I have come to know so well, the sun of children going away on sidewalks, of storekeepers taking their wives to the bus. Damn this balcony. Damn this kitchen. Damn all the butchers and priests. Damn, damn, damn . . . so easy to be negative. I read about Mexico and the volcanic drought spilling spiders from the mouth of Malcolm Lowry. Horribly depressing and deep, although written in the haze of a very expensive agony, an aesthetic pain. The worst of it is they say the whole thing is autobiographical. Suppose it couldn't be much else. Who would write about such a soggy life unless his own pores were jammed with the pus that later appears as paint?

"Really can't complain about the afternoon. The spring sun sent everything into a pleasant blur the way only alcohol can in the winter months."

"Charybdis, I turned you into a goddess with breasts of chain mail and fish hooks rustling in your vulva as you walked through the late Apache light along the promenade above the beach in Scilla. Swishing in velvet skirts and silver bracelets. Little did I know you were really a stonemason. On another beach, the black sand of Stromboli, as the night turned cool, and the acid was coming on, you pounded one rock with another and said, 'This is all I need.'

"The chronicle of my madness now sits before me like a spent candle. I gaze at patterns and wonder what it must have felt like to flow like that. I have shadows dripping from my eyes. Cars are parked outside my window, and if they are parked again like that tomorrow, if dinner still crawls onto my fork and down my throat like the night before, if sleep still comes around every evening like a bureaucratic fool, why go on? Suicide reasserts itself with astonishing vigor. It seems only when I think of imminent death does my mind hone itself into something that can be swung about my head."

There was of course the official attempt on Easter Monday, when I set out for the Jacques Cartier Bridge in the dying sunlight of the afternoon. Once I had decided I was going to kill myself in an hour or so, I enjoyed an immense peace of mind. As I rode the Métro out to Papineau station, I looked clear through the eyes of the other passengers with the incisive superiority of knowing what they didn't know, as they commuted back and forth on the rails of their banal lives. I was a madman on a train. I felt like standing up and crying out, "Feast your eyes on an intense and fully alive human being who will be dead tonight. You are getting the final glimpse of a beautifully wasted soul." It must have been in my eyes, because the other passengers seemed to look at me with a mixture of fascination and fear.

Out of the Métro, I walked through the squat underworld of lady wrestlers and bamboo pimps that live by the Jacques Cartier Bridge. I passed by the agency of cabaret artists on St. Catherine Street and wondered if I could solve my problems by becoming a male stripper. How many times had I passed by that store window and poured out my closet ambitions in silence as I gazed at posters of cabaret flesh? How often did I fantasize about going in there on the pretext of writing an article, "Notes from the Sexual Underground." This time the urge was stronger because of my imminent death. What could I lose? The shop was like a circus passing through town for a one-night stand. I wanted to become part of it, to stare out instead of in.

I looked through the window, and although it was past six, the light was on and a woman sat at a desk in the back. Comptroller of flesh, no doubt. A black hag guarding the gates of the unknown, knitting her typewriter, but secretly communing with a private army of lavender minnows in the St. Lawrence. I decided I was more ready for the bridge than for the hag.

To get there I cut across a barren field dotted with scraggly municipal trees. It sloped up to the road that led to the bridge. When I got to the top, I tried to cross to the other side, but the cars were thick and fast. I waited and waited and still no opening without the risk of getting killed. Bonked by a Chevrolet—that wouldn't do. I wanted to be on the other side of the bridge, the west side, facing upstream toward the city center. I had always imagined my suicide taking place on the west side, but I decided that if I was going to get fussy about which side of the bridge I would use, then I wasn't serious. So I started along the east side. In retrospect it seems logical that I fantasized about doing it facing upstream, because it was closer to home and mother and civilization. I would be facing all that, performing in front of it. The downstream side meant turning my back on it, surrendering to a river on its way to an ocean big enough to drown me, lose me and forget me. None of these inquiries into my motives occurred to me at the time. A bridge is a bridge, I thought. It shouldn't make an ounce of difference which side you jump from. We're not here for the view.

The view, however, was magnificent. The sunset had turned the city skyline pink. Behind it Mount Royal emerged as a soft, generous swell, a ripe silhouette promising a lush interior to anyone who cared to slide a scalpel along the horizon. I walked along the sidewalk on the wrong side of the bridge. Below there was pavement for the longest time, as the arc of the bridge rose higher and higher. Every few yards I stopped to look over the edge, calibrated the distance to impact in feet, stories, seconds.

The pavement was a surefire bet. Splat. As final as a subway car, with less public inconvenience. But that wouldn't have the glamour of a real bridge jump. It would be more like a building jump. The bridge doesn't really start until the water's edge. A bridge jump should take place from dead center.

The wind was perfectly cold. I was only a third the way across, still in the pubescent stage of suicide. Adventure lay ahead, and my heart was stirred by the possibility that this wasn't just fiction but a prelude to an event. In the end, none of us who have gone beyond the battle for subsistence in a society of waste seek anything but an eternal vision of ourselves sailing through our own slip in history. The smart ones never look back.

The pavement became water. Mustn't jump near the bank. Can't give myself a fighting chance of swimming to shore. What if I survived the freezing water and made it to shore only to find I could not climb up the cement embankment? No matter how sincere my desire to die, I knew that once I hit the water, if I was still conscious, the instinct to live would take hold. I would struggle to survive. Suicide isn't an irrational act, a mad act. To succeed, the individual, who is both murderer and victim, must be supremely rational—well balanced enough to play chess against himself and win. He must check out all the exits in advance. I knew that my plan was encumbered by two possible disasters from the outset: first, that I would botch the job, and second, that I would succeed but have regrets in the final moment before death.

I reached the center of the bridge. Then something started to happen. The world, this world of cement and steel, was turning into a marvelous desert, the marzipan kingdom. It took on a storybook quality, a Noddy book. Everything began to move more slowly, until I could touch history in its crystalline form. Time stopped. Everything was to be expected. The gaps between things had widened until there were only spaces.

It was getting colder. A ship came into view, steaming upstream and heading directly for the middle of the bridge. The appearance of the boat opened up a whole new set of alternatives. I could jump right away, before the boat got too close, and drown before it had a chance to catch up. I could jump near the boat, giving myself a chance to be rescued. Or I could jump onto the boat's metal deck, which would probably mean instant death—more instant than plopping into the water, and more fitting than dropping off a building. If, on the other hand, I waited until the boat passed under me, the entire moment would slip by. Time would start up again, and there would be no more chance of committing suicide that day, or for a long time to come. I had an audience with the abyss. It would move under me and I would have a split second in which to act.

So why didn't I do it?

Because my mind was as clear and full as the rising moon.

Because I no longer cared about any of the things that had driven me to the brink. About it, about *her*.

The swordfish and the girl were miles away. They were unaware. They weren't anywhere, because for once I was here instead of wishing myself elsewhere. I could suffer in the cold green swell, a hero to myself. Or I could accept defeat and sink back into the city's lap. That seemed much more attractive. I looked forward to the warm beery smell of taverns and strip joints, hocus-pocus shops, shadows behind the circus tent, carnies waving their candy-striped cocks around the fair. I felt extraordinary peace of mind. I clung to life as to a cup of hot chocolate.

What about the girl? She was around the corner sniff-ing coke, ripening her palms with a new piece of stick and winking back at me over her shoulder, just enough to keep the flame alive. But on the bridge she was nowhere to be seen. I was alone in my cosmic toytown, and the ship passed below like a toytown ship, inching past the railing of the bridge. It sailed right by me, or rather through me, turning my soul with it as though they were joined by gears. As the ship passed under and out of sight, I realized that the girl was forgotten. I was one with the world.

LIMBO

"*No more words!* Shouts, drums, dance, dance, dance, dance!"
–Rimbaud, *Une saison d'enfer*

I GAVE MYSELF UP to the streets and was passed through the arms of strangers. I practiced submission in basement rooms. And I developed an addiction to drums. Just weeks after Cléo moved to Toronto to live with her musician, I found myself taking up a musical instrument for the first time in my life. It sounds like a transparent ploy, but it was coincidence, albeit a fishy coincidence, the kind that gets sucked through a loophole in the law of probability, carried on a riptide of unconscious motives. Or something along those lines. The point is, my timely infatuation with drums was unpremeditated. I succumbed to the spell of the instruments even before I heard them, from the first moment I saw them set out onstage, like succulent totems, before a concert at the Université de Montréal in the fall of 1975.

They weren't ordinary drums. They were *djembes* in the West African style, hand drums carved in a bell shape that tapered down to a flared tail, with a goatskin head stretched under a rim of hammered metal. From the front of each hung a steel ring, knotted with a red sash. The instruments were arranged like polished chess pieces, waiting to be played.

The lights went down. A musician appeared and walked over to the drum at center stage. He was a wiry figure in a blue-striped sailor's shirt. He looked like a pirate, with fierce eyes and wild hair, Gallic features that were chiseled and hollowed like the drums, a face tattooed by experience. He had the haunted look of someone who had worked too long as a guide in the heart of darkness.

Going down on one knee, he picked up the drum and turned it over as if it were a strange object that he had found on a beach. He brought a palm down softly in the middle. It made a dark, padded thump. He hit it again, with more force, and produced a different sound altogether, a throaty boom that went right through the sternum. Laying the drum on the floor, the man then straddled it, and began working over the skin in an improvised series of false starts until clear shapes began to emerge: woodblock cuts with sharp right angles, round pops, wet slaps, metallic cracks and flurries of bell-like notes chiming off the rim.

You could feel the drum warming under his hands. Then, as if deciding it was time to move from foreplay to intercourse, he stood up, strapped the sash around his waist in a lightning move, and began to play. He sank into a rich, articulate rhythm. Drumbeats swirled through the room like a cloud of bees. Roving the stage, the pirate collated the sounds, shuffling and splitting them, until he had the music moving around the room with the precision of a remote-controlled plane. When he found the sweet spot, he stopped in his tracks, and with his eyes focused on a particular point in space, he massaged the rhythm until a deep wave of resonance welled up in the sound, a subterranean drone that fluxed through the room.

I didn't notice the other musician come onstage. But when I heard what he was playing—a melodic pattern spelled out in primary colors—I thought it must be coming from a guitar or keyboard. I looked up to see a tiny, androgynous Haitian playing a row of four conga drums. He wore a lime-green T-shirt and a beatific smile. Looking over at him, the pirate launched into an angry solo, violating the rhythm with manic detours. Unfazed, the Haitian simply held the beat, raising its intensity in meticulous increments, as if tuning a calibrated dial.

The pirate played like a man possessed. He seemed to be doing everything in his power to throw the other drummer off. But the Haitian just cocked his head in mock appreciation and smiled, serene as a prince, while continuing to up the ante, moving his arms in faster and wider arcs until they were a windmill blur, even though each beat still seemed deliberately placed, like a tile, and throughout it all he maintained an attitude of irreducible calm.

I was hooked. Afterwards I met the Haitian and arranged to take private lessons. He taught me a vocabulary of drum sounds and a repertoire of African, Latin and voodoo rhythms. I bought congas and commissioned the pirate, who once played with Charlebois, to make me a *djembe* out of Gatineau pine. I remember bringing it home on the bus, holding it with the pride of a parent cradling a newborn. The fresh goatskin, still coarse from where the fur had been shaved away, felt like warm bread to the touch.

A willing apprentice, I developed a rudimentary knowledge of percussion, enough to perform a few tricks. Outside my formal instruction, however, playing became an obsession. In the drum, I discovered an Aladdin's cave. Before playing, I always rubbed the skin, like the genie's lamp, until I could feel a blush of response. I learned that the skin, like the earth, was not flat but round, a cross between a gyroscope and a ball of clay. On the drum, I learned to shape waves, to beat them into clear angles of glass and steel, to surf the sound into a hum with a gliding fingertip, to carve out beveled cubes and pyramids. Skin, I discovered, had infinite depth.

Finally I had found a medium that placed no legal limit on delusion. In nature, I found it easy to converse with the weather. In fact, it was impossible not to. I could harden the sun and metabolize clouds. Certain rhythms would stiffen the wind or shift its direction. I could send vortices spiraling into the sky. A drum amplified the familiar paradigm of chaos theory—that the beating of a butterfly's wings can change events on the other side of the world. The problem was, I didn't really know what I was doing. The birds, which served as a sarcastic chorus, seemed to sense that. My attempts at musical communion with nature usually ended up replaying the same old drama: starting out in the Garden with a clean slate, then falling rudely from grace.

Playing with other musicians was a different story. I had friends in Limbo, the band being formed in Toronto by Ray, Cléo's new lover. They rehearsed in a concrete blockhouse behind a body shop, right next to the railway tracks in an industrial triangle known as the Junction. From the first time I played with them, there was never any doubt in my mind that I would join. It was like one of those westerns where a gunfighter becomes part of the gang without anyone saying much. The surprising thing is that I became enamored with Cléo's boyfriend, who sang lead. She was right: he was her mirror image. Playing with him was, metaphorically at least, like carrying on a long-distance romance with her. Though the connection remained unspoken, it produced a creative tension, which was recycled back into the music; most of the songs were originals, and they materialized out of whatever was in the air, the things between us.

In the overall sound of the band, I played a subliminal role. But from the beginning, I felt responsible for the magic. I learned something else about the drum that proved crucial: that the skin isn't just an object of percussion, but a membrane that works like an eardrum. I learned to touch the music through the skin, to feel the voices and guitars coming up through it like braille. I learned to take a voice in my hands, magnify it, polish it, sharpen its edges and paint it in jungle colors. I learned how to frig a guitar into a lather, to wrap keyboard notes in suede. I could freeze time and walk around inside.

It sounds megalomaniacal. But everyone in the band was doing it, even though none of us knew how it worked. The music had a life of its own, like the sea. We would play on it, sometimes well, sometimes badly, but it was always *there*, sending in bigger and bigger waves and asking us to go a little farther out each time.

Cléo and I observed each other from a distance. We maintained a cool friendship, but I continued to rendezvous with her in secret through the dreamscape of the music, replaying our lost tango in Stromboli. I'm sure it was happening more in my mind than hers, yet Cléo *was* the band muse. Three of the five band members were her ex-lovers, if you include an old romance with the bass player. Blair was a consummate bass player, a moody individual with a baritone voice and suicidal impulses that were held in check by a deft sense of humor. He was always threatening to quit. Max, the keyboard player, was an old friend from Montreal. He and Cléo were really an item, but he worshiped her in his own way. Max was the brains behind the band, the one who wrote the songs and drew up our strategy for world domination. That leaves the drummer, Bob, who was married with a kid and wasn't involved in any of the emotional subterfuge. He was the most easy-going person in the world, but ruthless onstage. He would ride the kit like a long-distance swimmer, and I'd look back and see him planing through the sweat that poured off his body. Bob was our Charlie Watts; he kept us honest.

Cléo loved the band at first. When a band starts out, it plays for its friends—its close friends—and during the early days, when the music was running on pure instinct, she basked in the attention. She would hit the dance floor by herself, wearing a shimmery top that clung to her body like an oil slick. I would catch her glances in nets of rhythm. Afterwards, in the dressing room, there was an unspoken tension between us, which she broke sometimes by acting demonstrative toward Ray, curling around him like a cat and pulling him into a corner with kisses. It was hurtful, but I taught myself to be immune. Anyway, they were the ones who had the relationship to protect, not me.

In time, Cléo came to resent the band. As we became more and more absorbed with each other, she could not compete. She was outside the clubhouse. Her lover, seeing his own image magnified in the spotlight, was soon lavishing more attention on it than on her. Inadvertently, I was helping to drive Cléo and her boyfriend apart. I couldn't help being tickled by the irony that I was spending more time with him than she was.

I think she and Ray had some sort of falling out during our stay at the club on the Yonge Street strip with the stainless-steel dance floor. It was run by a skinny gangster who ran around the place in a leopard-print vest with no shirt and looked like a young Roman Polanski. We became the house band there for a while. The gangster let us hop over the bar and help ourselves to free liquor every night after the place closed.

Ray and I were both pursuing Liane, a lithe waitress who danced around the place on roller skates wearing cutoffs and a halter top. I had a disappointing fling with her. She was a dreamgirl with a long aerobic body and silky blond hair, but like so many conventionally stunning women, she had the sort of glamour that loses its mystery when you get close. And her skin was kind of rubbery. I'm not sure what happened with her and Ray, but one night Cléo stalked out of the club after seeing them together backstage. He was leaning against the wall in that slinky pose of his, and Liane was sharing a cigarette with him, asking him what he did to keep his midriff so firm.

For a long time, Cléo didn't come to the gigs. When she started showing up again, it seemed more out of duty than desire. One summer when the band was playing up north in Parry Sound, she came up for the weekend. Ray had gone fishing with the owner of the local music store, who wanted to buy us a big new cube van with the band name on the side. Cléo and I went for a walk, taking the road that forks down under the railway trestle. She talked about the music, and how she liked the old songs better than the new stuff. We got to the water and sat down together on the grass bank. I asked how she was getting along with Ray.

She said she wasn't sure who he was anymore.

"It's like living with a stranger sometimes. He's so wrapped up with himself. Doing yoga for the band."

"He loves the yoga. But it could be worse. He could be out there getting wasted with groupies."

"Oh, I'm sure he's above all that."

I resisted an impulse to jump to Ray's defense, to say that he had become an ascetic, saving himself for the audience, that his sexuality had become a sacrament, that he would lash himself to the microphone and plug his ears rather than succumb to the sirens. Instead I asked if she still loved him.

"I don't know."

"So what are you going to do?"

She shrugged. "Go somewhere. I can't stand Toronto."

"Back to Montreal?"

"Maybe. I miss Montreal."

She lit a cigarette, and I rehearsed my next line a few times in my head, a non sequitur.

"Do you remember the first time we met?"

"Sort of. I remember I didn't like you much."

"Why not?"

"Oh, I don't know. Just an impression. You seemed so *égoïste.*"

"I didn't think much of you at first either. You seemed snobby. You had that drab student hair and you wore that untucked shirt, you know, that untucked khaki thing with the Vietnamese soldier on the back."

"I know. I can't believe I wore that."

It was odd. We had lived together for months before becoming lovers. After getting hired at the newspaper, I'd moved to Montreal with a girlfriend from Toronto. Our apartment was much too big for us, and Max introduced us to Cléo, who needed a place to live. She moved in and kept to herself, like a tenant. Then things deteriorated with my girlfriend, who kept hiding in the closet and threatening to commit suicide if I didn't step up my emotional commitment. Eventually she went back to Toronto, which left Cléo and me living on our own. It was a while before anything happened.

"What do you remember about the first night we slept together?" I asked.

"Not much."

"We were watching TV. You made popcorn. I slipped your socks off and started stroking your feet, and I worked my way up your legs, slowly."

"All I remember"—she laughed—"is how long it took you to get my clothes off."

"Oh, c'mon."

She laughed. "You took forever."

"I was *seducing* you."

"Well, you certainly took your time."

"Maybe if I'd known you were going to leave me, I would have have moved a little quicker."

There was an edge in my voice that I hadn't intended.

"Let's not start that again."

"But we've never talked about it."

"What's to talk about?"

"Why you left."

"Why I left? Look, you're so attached to this idea that you were left and betrayed, like this *victim.* Has it ever occurred to you it might have happened the other way around? Maybe you left me?"

"What are you talking about?"

"By the time I left, you were already gone. You'd been gone for ages."

"I was crazy. It's not the same. I didn't leave you, I left the planet."

"But before that. You were always off in your own world."

"You wanted it that way. You're the one who was worried about your independence."

"I was protecting myself."

"From what?"

"From becoming your little mistress who would tag along. You had this whole other life, all your *petites amies* at the paper. They'd phone for you, and I'd take their messages, and they'd have no idea who I was."

"You're exaggerating. Anyway, there was never anything serious."

"What about the one who called me when you were off in Toronto hanging out in the bath with what's-her-name? She said you'd phoned her and threatened to kill yourself if she didn't come to see you on the next train."

I couldn't remember anything like that.

"She was from Montreal?"

"Yes."

"English or French?"

"English."

"What was her name?"

"Oh, I don't know. Kate, Cathy, Carol . . . Carol."

"Carol . . . Jesus, I'd forgotten all about her."

"Well, back then you were ready to kill yourself over her, and she was asking me what to do."

"What did you tell her?"

"I said you were bluffing, that you probably just needed someone to help you get to sleep."

"Great. I could be dead now."

"I figured it wasn't my problem."

"Why did you stay with me as long as you did if things were so bad?"

"I don't know." Cléo sighed and lay back on the grass. Then she turned to me with a sadness in her eyes that I hadn't seen since we were together. "I guess I was still attached. And I felt I owed it to you. You'd given me something I never had before."

"A trip to Italy?"

"Fuck off."

"It was a joke. What did I give you?"

"I don't know. This sounds corny, but you made me realize I could be beautiful. I'd never even tried to be attractive before. I'd always felt so . . . *moche.*"

"The good feminist."

"Partly. But I don't think I'd ever met anyone who cared about how I looked."

"I worshiped you. That was a mistake."

"I didn't mind."

We sat in awkward silence. The sun went behind a cloud and a breeze rose off the water. I put my arm around Cléo and gave her a sexless hug. She said I was a good person and she'd always be fond of me.

It was all wrong. I wanted to kiss her on the mouth, to pull her to the ground and wrestle everything back into place. But I didn't have the anger or the impulse, just an abstract desire. And, now that nothing mattered quite so much as the band, I also felt bound by a fidelity to Ray. The stakes between Cléo and me were even now: we were both in a position to betray him.

"We could always get back together," I said. "That would get them talking."

"*Ooh la la. Quel scandale.*"

A cabin cruiser came by. People drinking cocktails on the rear deck waved to us the way people on boats always do.

"Let's go back," she said.

My courting of Cléo through the music crystallized into a conceit. The ballads that struck me as Cléo-specific gradually fell out of favor. The repertoire was always changing, and like the rest of the band, I began to find performance more seductive than romance. The audiences grew. We acquired trucks and patrons. We had roadies who rolled massive spliffs and blew smoke into our mouths between sets. We played in places like Halifax, Cleveland and Wasaga Beach. A New York promoter who worked with the Rolling Stones groomed us for the Big Time. He showed up in his Stones tour jacket and helped us persuade the bank to lend us a ridiculous sum of money. We developed an elaborate concept: the band and the audience were amnesiac survivors of nuclear holocaust, the show was set in the ruins, and the songs would take us back through the nightmare, recovering our memories and landing us safely on the other side. Affecting a post-nuclear style, we scorched our instruments and burned holes in our costumes. Ray let his kinky black hair grow into white-guy dreadlocks. We went onstage in makeup with our bodies wrapped in colored electrical cords.

We were crazy. But insanity finds safety in numbers, and the band evolved into a kind of corporate delusion. Whenever it looked as though it was going to break up, or break down for lack of funds, someone came along and gave us another wad of money, or a gig, or something. The whole thing seemed to be out of our hands, everything but the music. That was the only world that made sense, the time we spent onstage.

On the road, a kind of unreality set in. The van would come by early in the morning. You'd step inside, into the rock'n'roll pod, music pouring from the tape deck, the side door slides shut, someone hands you a joint, and then it's off to Ohio or Quebec or one of those northern towns where half the audience is stoned on some bizarre drug like Ritalin.

Several years went by, just like that. Personnel changed. We acquired Garrett, a lead guitarist from Cleveland with a kerosene voice who took rock'n'roll more literally than the rest of us. He was always on the verge of the Big Time—he had played with all kinds of famous people—but was one of those musicians who was too good for his own good. He didn't know when to stop, or how to compromise, or where to draw the line between life and art, or why. He had to do everything for real, as if the world was going to end before the last song in the third set. He was always breaking guitar strings in mid-epiphany, and juggling girlfriends and investing his liver with more hard liquor than it could possibly amortize.

Garrett taught us how to behave. With him, we learned to feel at home in hotel rooms that were in an organic state of decomposition. I remember once, at about three in the morning, we were sitting in one of these rooms sharing a bottle of rye handed to us by Pete-from-down-the-hall, who had passed out on the floor. Garrett disappeared into the closet and came out hauling a massive tangle of bedsprings, which was attached to all the junk growing out of the walls. He kept pulling on it until he was dragging a great trail of plaster and debris around the room. It looked like he was unraveling the hotel.

Things got out of hand during a week-long winter

gig in Kingston, in a motel on the frozen edge of Lake Ontario. We all came down with the flu, the kind that makes you mentally ill before you realize you have it. They had booked us three to a room. There was virtually no heat in the rooms, and no hot water because the Ice Capades were staying there and they all took showers at once. One morning I lost my temper with a thermostat that wasn't responding and gave it a thump with my fist.

"Why dontcha use the hockey stick?" said Bob, handing me one that Ray took on the road for pick-up games.

I jammed the butt end hard into the thermostat and felt the glass shatter and the insides come loose. It felt so good I gave it another couple of whacks. Blue sparks leaped out of the wall. If you could get this high on the death rattle of a mere thermostat, I thought, no wonder Keith Moon got addicted to the thrill of throwing TV sets through hotel windows.

Ray, who didn't know his mind was already fucked by the early stages of the flu, went out to play some shinny hockey one afternoon in a park and collided head-on with another player. He staggered out of the rink with a ten-stitch cut. After he got himself sewn up and bandaged, we were in the middle of dinner at a health-food restaurant when his wound began to bleed into his eggplant casserole. The table of vegetarians next to us were visibly disturbed by the intrusion of rock'n'roll gore into their wholesome surroundings.

I agreed to drive Ray back to the hospital to get a bigger

bandage. Now I was getting the flu, although I didn't know it yet, and my mind was starting to go pleasantly woozy. I backed the van firmly into a parked Bobcat. The bumpers locked, and I dragged the car a good thirty feet trying to get it unstuck. Ray, who tended to take over in situations like this, got out a crowbar and tried to pry the two vehicles apart, without success. Finally he just dropped the tire iron, said "I'm getting outta here" and ran after a taxi. By then a small crowd of spectators had gathered on the sidewalk trying to piece it all together: who was the man with a tire iron in his hand and blood streaming down his face, and how could such a minor collision have such grisly consequences?

Ray came back from the hospital with a much bigger bandage. That night, standing at the microphone with a mane of black dreadlocks bound in a gauze headband, he looked like a guerilla fresh from some exotic torture. I think the audience assumed it was all part of our post-nuclear scenario. It was a rocky night. Just before we were about to go on, one of the roadies accidentally dropped the electronic guitar tuner—the Tuning God, as we affectionately called it—into an ice bucket full of water. He fished it out and fiddled with the knobs, trying to get it to work.

"I think it's wasted, man," he said finally, handing it to Ray.

Ray looked at it dumbly as though someone had just handed him a run-over dog.

We had begun to lose our grip; a chain reaction had set in.

When we got back to Toronto, Ray went home to discover that Cléo was gone. She had moved back to Montreal. The band, meanwhile, was not long for this world. The bank was moving in on us. Our New York contacts continued to offer moral support, but they kept telling us we needed patience. The band couldn't wait. It was melting down of its own accord. We lost the truck, then the equipment, then the rehearsal space by the railway until there was nothing left of Limbo but a toxic puddle of financial complications. It was not supposed to end like this. According to Garrett, we were going to play well into the apocalypse.

Without the band, I was adrift. I believed in nothing. The month of March had come around once again, and I had a desire to take one more excursion into the void, to hurl myself, like Rimbaud, over the edge of the flattening earth—"I shall return with limbs of iron, dark skin, a furious eye . . . Women take care of these ferocious invalids returned from hot countries." Like the women who bathed Ulysses and rubbed his body with olive oil. That would be something to look forward to.

I traveled south with a drum.

Through my faded connections in the International, which served as a first-rate travel agency, I looked up contacts in the Lesser Antilles—in Antigua, Guadeloupe and Martinique. The French islands, I was pleased to learn, were volcanic. I told anyone who would listen that I wasn't coming back.

THE HOLE

EASTERTIME in Antigua. A hot blue sky. Gold pastures of biblical sheep tended by Rastamen who roamed diagonally across the land, oblivious of roads. I stayed with a friend of a friend in a two-room house on a country road a mile from the beach: Ube, a gentle black man with a beard who was growing new dreadlocks under a maroon beret. He played bass in a local reggae band, which admitted me as an outpatient percussionist.

Practicing with the band in his small stucco house, I would stare at the palm frond waving like a large fin outside the window. One morning we played Bob Marley's "Rat Race" over and over, learning it off the record while smoking vast quantities of ganja. There were times when I found myself freefalling through the bottomless spaces in the one-drop beat. But I'd look up at the drummer's Buddha smile, which seemed to say, "Don't worry, that's what it's for," and in the tap of his cowbell or the swish of a cymbal, I could always find a handhold.

Outside the tourist enclave, there is no anonymity for a white man in the tropics. People wondered what I was up to. One afternoon I was walking down the road when I heard the low thumping of a drum. It was coming from five Rastas on a hillside. Men with onyx eyes and sunburst dreads, who seemed to be riding the hillside like the prow of a ship. They reminded me of the black angels in García Lorca's *Gypsy Ballads*, "angels with hearts of oil and long and braided tresses." (I was later corrected on the difference between men and angels by another Rastaman, who claimed to live on nothing but honey, which he drank from a rum bottle. He pointed to a horse appearing over the crest of a hill and said, "*That* is an angel.")

As I walked past the five Rastas, the man beating the drum, a piece of cowhide staked to a slim hollowed log, stopped playing and hailed me. "What is your mission?" he asked.

"Oh, just going down the road."

"You go to the beach."

"No."

"Then where you *go*, mon?"

"Nowhere."

Immediately I felt the entire weight of white existential decadence on my shoulders. The man's eyes and those of his friends stared right through me and on into infinity.

"You can't *go* nowhere, mon," said the drummer. "You go one way or you go de other. But a man can't go nowhere. Iniquity is a dread place. Are you a fallen angel?"

How I would have loved to shout out, "Yes, fallen and still falling, dizzy, delirious, lying with the devil, flowering with evil and burning sulfur."

My reply, which I don't remember, was noncommittal. Something about taking a stroll.

Easter was a holy season for the Rastas in Antigua, who regarded airplanes and electricity as the work of the devil and herb the food of God. They had little patience for people just wandering around with no mission. People go one way or the other, to Jah or Satan. The alternatives were always clear, as tangible as sun and rain. And when Iniquity stalked the island, it was obvious to everyone all at once, like the epidemic of colds that struck on Good Friday. The longer I stayed among the Rastas as a foreign wanderer who flew in from nowhere and didn't know where he was going, the more I sensed a creeping suspicion about my morals.

On the Saturday night just before I left the island, Ube walked with me to the Admiral's Inn. It was the first time he'd been there in a year. After being caught balling a white tourist's wife, he had been told to clear off and never come back. For him, our Saturday-night excursion was a daring venture into enemy territory. He walked tall and talked loud. It was a sad, drunken evening. Ube was so self-conscious, so arrogantly sure that his mere presence in the Admiral's Inn would cause a scandal, that it did.

As soon as he was past the stone gates of the old harbor

fortress that now serves as a luxury hotel, he was picking a fight. Before long, some of the local boys, teenagers trying to act older, taunted Ube that there was something sexual going on between him and me. Otherwise, they said, why would he lodge a white man in his house? Ube just made it worse by screaming that love between men is God's love but there is one thing he would never do and that is ball someone in the ass because the ass is meant for shitting *period.* His shouts rose above the sound of a dinky steel band playing watered-down calypso for the dancing tourists, who pretended to ignore us.

As Ube and I walked home, the road was silent and the sky was crisp with stars. Despite everything, we felt good, and Ube remained proud. But when we reached the house, we found the door and windows had been forced open. Inside nothing had been touched except for my shoes and his bed. My shoes had disappeared. And his bed . . . it had been swung out diagonally from the wall so that it pointed directly at the spot where my shoes had been. Ube was heartbroken. Someone he knew, someone familiar with the shoes, had broken into his house.

"This the first time something like this ever happen to me," he said, tears in his eyes. "I never feel so bad. It not even my house, you know. I don't own the house. Maybe if it was my house I have a different feeling. But why dem take your shoes? I could see dem taking a guitar or a tape recorder. But a pair of shoes? Tis a dread ting to happen, mon."

I assumed it was a warning, a symbolic theft, some amateur sorcery, perhaps. It made me feel sad and very white, but I can't deny that it gave me a certain frisson, as if I had been touched by voodoo. I would miss the shoes, however, especially when it came time to climb the volcano in Martinique.

Stromboli had left a permanent shadow across my imagination, a scorch mark. Over the years, the volcano would surface in dreams, the kind that transport you to a place more real than the waking world. But my attachment to the island was not sentimental; I no longer associated it with the end of a romance. Instead, the place itself had become a clandestine lover, stealing into my room in the middle of the night.

In Guadeloupe, I wasted no time in visiting La Soufrière, an active volcano rising from the western wing of the island, which has the shape of a butterfly. As volcanoes go, it was a stubby affair, in desperate need of an eruption. It was no Stromboli. An easy climb took me to the summit, a moonscape of sulfur yellow rock bearded with crimson, orange and rust-colored ferns. Here and there, water gurgled up through lukewarm clay, reluctant spasms of a volcano that had seen better days. The Muzak of impotence. While I watched and listened, trying to form a connection, I was annoyed by the presence of a French tourist who had sought the safety of my company during the climb, a pudgy, middle-aged man wearing only a swimsuit. He couldn't stop talking about the danger of the place. As the sun sank lower and a cool breeze picked up, he kept telling me we should leave. I ignored him, hoping that he would leave me alone with my volcano, such as it was, and eventually he did.

Before going back down the mountain, I stared at the bubbling clay for a few minutes, spoke some sacred gibberish to the earth and prayed for an eruption. Two months later there would be a fairly decent eruption of La Soufrière, enough to force an evacuation but not enough to get anybody hurt.

That spring in Guadeloupe, I stayed on the other side of the island from the volcano. Françoise lived alone in a house a few miles in from the coast. She was older than me, in her thirties, a French-Moroccan teacher who had Arabic features and a brisk manner. Those days there was nothing untoward about asking for a few days' hospitality from a total stranger, as long as the guest had references. But neither Françoise nor I were active in the International, so it all seemed a bit tenuous. I spent a couple of nights at her house, while she tried to figure out what to do with me.

Françoise was the kind of woman who liked to know what was going on at all times. Suddenly she had a strange man in her house who spoke cautious, accented French. She talked with that impatient, aggressive edge that Parisians adopt when they are on the phone, unable to suspend their disbelief that there is someone at the other end. From the moment I showed up at her door, beneath her vivacious cordiality I could see the back of her mind clicking away, as if there had been some silly bureaucratic mistake. But part of her was intrigued. And she liked the idea that I traveled with a drum.

One night she took me to see a friend, an older man named Arto, who was reputed to be the best drummer on the island. Arto and I sat together and drummed in the dusty yard beside his house. He had amazing hands. Purring over the skin like a hummingbird's wings in the beginning, then cutting the rhythm with fierce, unpredictable gunshot cracks that sounded like they would wake up the entire island. We volleyed back and forth, but he called the shots.

An old woman in an apron did a lewdly comic dance while Françoise watched Arto in a controlled rapture. I imagined his hardened drummer hands working her body, blurring her clit with complicated orgasms. It was obvious they had a history together. You could see it in her eyes. Later she admitted as much but said it was over. "He's hopeless. Shows up at two in the morning, then you don't see him for a week."

It was almost that late when we got home. Françoise paced about the living room, shivering. "It's so cold," she said, as if I should do something about it. People who live in the tropics have strange ideas about the cold. Suddenly she was standing close to me, her arms folded around bare shoulders, her eyes looking away. I noticed her perfume, a thread of musk, and imagined the sex waiting to happen, my face in her dark hair, hashish-sweet, her body under the black dress.

Stupidly, I told her it wasn't all that cold. She shook her head and walked away. I could have put my arms around her, kissed her. She would have liked that, the aggressive approach, like one of the men from the island. She was probably one of those tough women who was just waiting for someone strong enough to let her crack, to unravel. But I wasn't sure. You wouldn't want to miscalculate with a woman like that, she'd eat you for breakfast. So I took the safe route. "Here, I'll warm you up," I said, rubbing her back in an asexual way. She laughed, exasperated, like someone stuck on a bad blind date. I still have no idea whether she wanted to be seduced or left alone. But the middle ground was definitely a mistake.

The next morning, she offered to find another place for me to stay. Nothing personal, she just needed space. She knew some friends down the road who would be perfect. She said, "They're not in the Organization. I think they used to be Maoists. But they won't mind. They like everybody."

That's how I came to stay with Marie-Claire, her husband and her eight-year-old daughter in the house overlooking the valley. It was a fine old cottage with a broad verandah. The breeze came up from the ocean, adopting the warm scent of sugar cane from the fields. And down in the valley the air was articulate with the odors of almond, mango and maracudja. Marie-Claire's husband was an architect who worked in town and didn't seem to mind what she did with me in the afternoons. So we went for long walks and made lemon-grass tea from the citronelle leaves that grew beside the verandah.

The first time that she took me on a tour through the valley and named all its secrets, I felt we had both been there since childhood, although we had scarcely met. It was paradise, and Marie-Claire, at home with the breeze in her long Spanish skirts, was its mistress. Each time she introduced me to some new exotic vegetation, it was like meeting a close acquaintance. And each time I would ask her if it was edible—*Est-ce que ça se mange?*—a question she found increasingly funny. Toward the end of the walk, we stopped for a moment on a grassy slope that led up to the house. Touching her bare shoulders and sun-warm hair, I asked her with a naiveté that only my childlike French would allow me to carry off: *"Est-ce que ça se mange aussi?"*

She smiled. "*Peut-être plus tard.*"

During that first walk through the valley, and all the others that came after, we followed the same ritual. First we would stop at the *calebassier*, a tree with no leaves and a spray of spidery branches supporting fruits the size of melons that were perfectly round and bright green. So spherical they looked like balls on a Christmas tree, except bigger. It seemed a shame to pick them, the way they could sprout from nothing, without even a stem, and hang with all that weight from such slender branches. But Marie-Claire gave me a boost and I reached into the blue sky and pulled one down, and we carried it like a smooth baby while we continued our walk. The calbasses were inedible, but scraped and dried they made fine gourds.

Farther on, we visited the wild orange tree, small and alone in a field. Its perfume found us from yards away. We took three of its fruit, and as our fingers tore away the peel, the bitter scent filled our minds like a narcotic. Later we walked through purple stalks of sugar cane and hid inside their jungle of lime leaves like children lost in tall grass, while higher up on the hillside we saw a peasant woman stooped over a yam patch and an old man chaining a goat to a bush. They both looked down on us with smiles that made me shudder.

We came to where the canefield had been cut to stubble and a black boy lay on his back, gleaming half-naked in the sun, slowly sucking on the sweet white fiber of a cane stick held between raised knees. He was oblivious to us. We skirted nervously around a bull that blocked the footpath. Farther ahead, the valley narrowed and the path became stony. Marie-Claire led me to the edge of the forest that covered the hillside. There, among the distracted odors of almond and fern, she showed me a tree with an amazing fruit. Shaped like a teardrop, it had a hard-ridged skin streaked with orange and crimson flames. She told me it was cocoa. That made me wonder about all the sins of civilization, to think that someone had found the time and inclination to convert this fruit into chocolate, although Marie-Claire and I ate a lot of chocolate, especially at the beach, where we would wash it down with big cheap bottles of sweet lemonade called Royal Soda.

The beach was a bit of a drive. It was at the very tip of the island, a narrow spine of land with a Caribbean cove of pink coral sand on one side and the Atlantic thrashing against rocks on the other. You got to the cove by a long footpath through thornbushes. It was a nude beach, and that was how we saw each other naked for the first time. Marie-Claire acted as though it was no big deal. When we got home, we would wash off the salt in the open-air shower, and even after we were dry there was no rush to get dressed. In the living room, she would stand on the cool tile floor and apply raspberry lotion to her skin. She had a long, smooth body with simple lines like a Matisse, lines that seemed unbroken by the shy roundness of her breasts and hips; straight brown hair that fell past her shoulders; quiet gray eyes and a delicate, unrevealing mouth. But she had very large hands, heavy, blunt-fingered hands that did not look at all like the rest of her.

We spent many a day at the beach and made no secret of it. She kept telling me that her husband wouldn't mind. True, Pierre expressed not a hint of hostility toward me. He was a tall, gaunt man with long hair, a beard and a Gallic nose. He looked a bit like Jesus. Each night we all ate dinner together and drank red wine. Every meal would end with cheese. Pierre would always take a large slice of Brie, and as he devoured it, he'd grin and say how good it was and why didn't I have some more. He and I got along quite well really, talking music and politics. I tried to feel guilty about taking advantage of his hospitality, but he wouldn't hear of it. I think he found me amusing. We would sit on the verandah and listen to Pink Floyd, which always seemed serenely in tune with the sounds of the valley as the sun dropped and the orchestra of tree frogs and insects tuned up for the night. I would go to bed alone in a small blue pup tent beside the house.

One night, Marie-Claire and I camped at the beach with her daughter. She said Pierre would understand—for all he cared we could have been going on a Sunday school picnic. Once her daughter was asleep, we lay on the beach and stared at the stars without talking. It was a cold night. We undressed each other under a sleeping bag and made love in slow, quiet secrecy.

We stole other opportunities, whenever we were alone. One day we met in a second-floor apartment left empty by a friend in town. I was close to climax when she said she might be ovulating. She phrased it halfway between a warning and an invitation. With the traffic noise drifting up through the louvered windows, our bodies slowly combined in the sweat of the afternoon, our arousal exaggerated by the suspense. I skated the brink of orgasm for a long time while we searched each other's eyes, looking for some affirmation, but she left it up to me, coaxed her hand down the small of my back, until I fell surrendering inside her.

That changed things. A while later, we were going for one of our walks in the valley when she stopped by the cocoa tree and told me she might be pregnant. Calmly, evenly. I looked at her with transparent fear, which I tried to convert to open-minded intrigue when I realized that her own feelings were more ambivalent.

The pregnancy turned out to be a false alarm. Perhaps she had just been testing me. I don't know. We didn't fight about it, but we were never as close after that.

Spring slipped indiscernibly into summer in the valley, where time was not a seasonal affair. The only visible change was that the mangoes ripened and all the cane was cut to stubble. No matter what the season, something was always ripening in the valley. Marie-Claire said it was a shame I couldn't stay until Christmas, when heavy rains would produce a wild crop of hallucinogenic mushrooms. She and her husband both asked me to stay, although I sensed that the daughter was relieved when I said I was moving on.

There was one last walk in the valley, which was now littered with mangoes. Each of the tall *manguiers*, with its mass of dark-green leaves, had shed more fruit than anyone would ever eat. Marie-Claire picked one up and peeled back the thick skin and ate it as we walked. She stopped and handed it to me. I ate some and passed it back. "*Il en reste toujours*," she said, and stood there watching me with cat's eyes while she sucked on the mango, raking her teeth over the orange flesh until there was nothing left but the slippery fiber around the pit. "*C'est fini, la mangue,*" she said with a squinting smile.

We made a final excursion to the pink sand beach, spent a few untalkative hours naked under an overcast sky. Late in the afternoon, we went back to the house and washed off the salt with a shriek of icy rainwater from the cistern. We dried ourselves slowly, her raspberry scent like cream in the air, then stood by the mirror for a long time before touching. Our skin still cool from the shower, we made love on a mattress by the window. Afterwards, we both cried softly to ourselves, each feeling betrayed by the other's emptiness. As we lay there, we felt a shadow pass through our bodies, a shudder of air, and it began to rain.

The next day Pierre offered to drive me across the island to the airport. I said the bus stop at the corner of the coast highway would be fine. Marie-Claire and their daughter came along for the ride. As they dropped me off, Pierre told me to come back and visit any time, and Marie-Claire reminded me to write. They drove off waving, over the hill, and as I watched the dust settle on the road behind them, a boy came by selling drinks and cigarettes. I hadn't smoked for a year, but without really thinking about it, I bought some unfiltered Gitaines. I opened the pretty blue pack with the silhouette of the gypsy dancer and lit one up. The tobacco smacked my lungs like a flat blade, a raw wind on exposed bone. It made me feel anonymous and dizzy. I loved it. It gave a taste to the sadness. I was leaving home again, and I could feel the smoke erasing the world behind me.

Martinique was two islands down, a short hop in a two-engine plane. Bouncing through turbulence, we climbed away from Guadeloupe and headed across open water. The next island down was Dominica, the place the newspaper had promised to send me before I disqualified myself. Banking sharply, the plane veered away from it, skirting the island's mountainous shore. I looked down, trying to decipher something out of the dark slopes, and thought about how strange it is that things turn out the way they do. Through the scratches of the Plexiglas window, I watched the plane's shadow sliding across the water as we continued on to Martinique. The island came up fast. The shadow passed over turquoise reefs, a narrow rim of black sand, and soon it was rippling across a maze of sharp green contours.

Aside from some mangrove swamps in the south, Martinique is a jumble of mountains and ravines. It is like a naive painting without perspective, a crayoned landscape of zigzags. The mountains climb, concertina-like, to a northern headland dominated by Mount Pelée, a volcano rising 4,583 feet out of the rainforest. Pelée erupted in 1902, killing some thirty thousand people and transforming the port of St. Pierre from the Paris of the Caribbean into an *antillaise* Pompeii. One of the town's only survivors was a convicted murderer awaiting execution in a dungeon.

Technically, Pelée is still active. From what I could gather, it seemed in no imminent danger of erupting. But its sheer presence, dominating the island, was intimidating enough. After the gentle, soft-edged charms of Guadeloupe, Martinique was a less patient paradise, an island of severe angles. André Breton called it "*la charmeuse des serpents*," the snake charmer.

In the island's capital, Fort-de-France, a frantic colonial town that seemed more French than Caribbean, I stay in an old apartment with a couple of middle-aged communists. They give me a copy of *Cahier d'un Retour au Pays Natal*, an epic poem by Martinique's Aimé Césaire. It reads like a rage of blood spit into the dust, the eloquently strangled cry of a man waking "*au bout du petit matin*" to find himself surrounded by the sleeping faces of thousands still dreaming the infernal dream. This is the poem that Breton stumbled across and adored, a voice that shrieks to make the spaces hum—"*le tam tam aveugle*"—the blind beat of a drum cracking open the night.

I sit in a room of austere mahogany antiques. There is a silver tea service that has never been used and a fishless aquarium full of brackish water and mossy rocks. From the window I can see across the hot tile roofs of the city to the rainforest, the green beginnings of volcanoes, the symmetrical maze of bumps, cones and warps that lead to

Mount Pelée. I watch two birds, one white and one black, intertwine flight lines, criss-crossing back and forth in crazy eights. The white bird is poetry; the black bird prophecy. Their paths unreel like silver lace spinning from a single sex; wheeling arcs high above the orange shingles, the dust, car horns and market smells; flying out of the town, above the knotted bric-a-brac of sweat and muscle, until they vanish into the mountains, continuing in my imagination, to the volcano's peak.

The two birds revive my faith in augury, and I pick up the pen to retrace their flight in the abstract. I struggle with words like gems in a flypaper brocade. A topaz here, emerald there. But they don't roll into their settings the way they should. My hands get gummy. The luster of the stones is quickly dulled. I despair for the picture that paints itself, the language that speaks as automatically as a meadow in a sleeping eye.

I want to relinquish writing, to give up on words, even the blank verse of the drum, compulsive calligraphy. I keep telling myself that the answer lies *out there*, at the island's apex.

From Fort-de-France, I traveled north to Ajoupa-Bouillon, a village not far from the volcano, and stayed with its Marxist mayor, who came highly recommended. Because there were not, after all, a great many elected officials in the International, he was something of a legend in the extreme left. Ajoupa is tucked into a lovely cleft of the jungled hills and gorges that wind down the slopes of Pelée. Each morning I awoke to a racket of birds and stepped out onto the terrace to gaze at the mountain. Its peak always attracted a mass of angry clouds, even out of the bluest sky, and some mornings I stared at it for hours, waiting to catch a glimpse of the summit. I swore I would climb it on the first clear day.

Luci insisted on driving me to the base of the volcano. She lived in the apartment beneath the mayor's, and we had slept together. It was the mayor's idea. It left him free to call over his whore, who responded to a coded signal from his outside light. If I went with Luci, he felt no compunction to share his whore or dig up another one for me. The mayor was a man of insistent courtesy.

Luci was older than me. She had a bold face with ravenous blue eyes and short blond hair that gave her more than a passing resemblance to Joan of Arc. She enjoyed sex and wanted more than I could possibly provide. But I was gentle, imbued with a porous sensitivity, and after she had been fucked around like a yoyo by the mayor whenever he was in the mood, she found me the closest thing to love she'd had since dropping her husband to jump into a futile affair several years earlier. I was beginning to take a dim view of sex in foreign countries. Sometimes it seemed the polite thing to do, like washing the dishes.

Luci packed me a lunch of cheese, fruit and chocolate, and we set out along the road that hairpins around the base of Mount Pelée, clinging to the edge of cliffs like mascara. She raced the car around those curves as though at any moment the road behind her might melt away into the abyss along with the ferns.

At Morne Rouge we stopped to pick up a hitch-hiker who was also headed for the volcano. He spoke no French and addressed us in English. Judging by his accent, I guessed he was Dutch or German: short light-brown hair, a neatly trimmed beard, wire-rimmed glasses.

"You are going to the mountain?" he asked. "This is the road to the volcano, yes? You can let me off?"

"*Oui, oui!*" said Luci. "You also climb the *montagne. C'est parfait.*" She turned to me. "You won't have to go alone, *mon cher*. You'll have a little friend."

This wasn't how I had imagined it at all.

As we approached the base of Pelée, another hitch-hiker flagged us down, a young Frenchman with a shock of carrot-colored hair and a face full of pimples. His scrawny frame was bent under an army rucksack. He was on a three-day leave from his military service, on his way to Macuba because he'd never been there and had nothing better to do. When he heard we were off to the volcano, he decided to change his plans and join the expedition. He said that was his original plan, but he didn't dare go alone because of the crevasses.

"*Bien, donc, vous pouvez tous monter ensemble,*" chirped Luci. "*C'est formidable comme ça. Voilà, on rencontre toujours des jeunes touristes.*" She was brimming with enthusiasm, as if each new hitch-hiker fulfilled some vision of a great gang of young tourists safely trekking up the mountain as happy as clams. More excited than we were, Luci dropped us at the foot of the mountain and, after mothering us with ample warnings, drove off, promising to return at five o'clock and call the police if we hadn't come down by six. The three of us stood together and stared at the mountain for not more than a minute. We couldn't see the summit, which was hidden behind a smaller peak that had to be climbed first. The path shot straight up this first slope, then disappeared.

The Dutch/German tourist gave the path a crisp gaze, then turned to us: "Do you want to go up quickly or slowly?"

I hardly heard him. My mind was elsewhere.

"Slowly," said the soldier.

"Well, I want to go up quickly."

The next thing I knew he was halfway up the first peak while we were still standing at the bottom. My sense of time had slipped away. There he was, far ahead, marching at a good civilized clip like someone late for work. I remember thinking I should have stopped him rushing ahead like that. Perhaps he didn't know it was dangerous—Luci's warnings about crevasses were all in French. But who was I to go telling strangers what to do? I didn't say anything. All I know is that one minute he was there and the next he was way the hell and gone.

I envied him. It would be more exciting to go alone.

But I was stuck with this funny-looking French kid who seemed to have trouble standing under the weight of his rucksack, never mind climbing a mountain. We started up the path at a slow pace, me in the lead and him scrambling behind. Having lost my shoes to voodoo, I was climbing in sandals, but had no trouble staying ahead. Every few hundred yards I stopped to let the French kid close up the slack, while still keeping him at a distance.

After two hours we reached the ridge that gave us our first look at the cone of the volcano itself. The ridge was a sheer cliff dropping hundreds of feet down to a curving valley, a caldera valley blown out by the last eruption. Rising on the other side was a symmetrical cone, coated with a smooth emerald furze. Not a single tree or bush marred the even texture of grass and moss. The top half of the peak was hidden by cloud. There were no clouds anywhere else. This ring of white mist around the cone was like a ceremonial veil, shielding an erogenous zone of the earth.

My companion went up the path to take pictures and I was left alone on the ridge. It was cool and still. At once I felt subject to a spell. There was a deliberate silence, soothed only by the hiss of air on the wings of swallows that circled the cone in spiral glides. Then I watched the mist slowly begin to rearrange itself until it finally slipped away, like a camisole, to reveal an immaculate green shape against the sky.

For a few long minutes I stared at the cone. Or rather it

stared at me. Displaying itself, naked and animate, a sex organ of the earth. The air seemed latent with recognition. And for a moment, as the wind died, I could feel some sort of pact pass between us, a grave complicity. Then the mist slipped its shroud back over the peak, like a blanket on a bird cage, and the communion was over. My red-haired companion reappeared, as if on cue. We sat on the ridge in silence and watched the mountain for some time, but the mist would not lift again.

In such a lucid silence, the scream was crystal-clear: a long, resonant shriek, the unmistakable sound of a man falling to his death. It came as a surprise, yet it seemed both timely and inevitable. After an unreasonably long pause, my companion and I turned to each other. Our eyes met. No, it wasn't just our imagination. We had both heard it.

"Sounds like our friend may have run into a little trouble," he said.

"That's what it sounds like."

"Maybe he's playing with the echoes."

"Maybe."

There had to be a less dramatic explanation than death. Besides, etiquette demands that one be found. So we both yelled. We yelled at the top of our lungs. But each time we stopped to listen, after the echoes faded there was no sound aside from the swallows' wings scything the air.

"He must have fallen into a hole," said the French kid.

"It seems incredible, but I guess it's possible."

I felt awkward, cornered by illicit emotions. We wondered what to do.

Finally I said, "There's nothing we can do but climb to the top and hope we meet him on the way. If we don't, we can assume he's in trouble or dead and we'll have to call the police when we reach the bottom."

I knew we wouldn't find our friend—we kept calling him that although neither of us knew him from the hole in the ground into which he had presumably fallen. That scream was a *hole* scream, the scream of a man who knows his death is imminent. No one could pretend with a scream like that. But I maintained an official concern for his life. It seemed the civilized thing to do. Rational concern for the life of a fellow human, even a total stranger, is compulsory. Even a corpse is given the benefit of the doubt, some perfunctory mouth-to-mouth resuscitation on the off-chance he might revive. To tell you the truth, I didn't really care if our friend was alive or dead. In fact—and this is most difficult to admit—I secretly *hoped* he had fallen to his death.

By the end of the afternoon, we returned to the foot of the mountain, slaked our thirst with a few bottles of beer at the café and waited for Luci to come with the car. We told our story to the café manager, who just shook his head and told us no one should climb the volcano without a guide because it's full of crevasses hidden by light ferns and grass.

Luci was horrified by our news. She bought us both

magnificent plates of coldcuts and salad and insisted we call the police at once. I phoned the station at Morne Rouge, but the officer at the other end claimed there was no one there and referred me to the police at St. Pierre. The St. Pierre station told me to call Morne Rouge. Finally the Morne Rouge police said they would come and meet us at the café. Half an hour later they phoned back and asked if we would mind coming down to visit them instead.

There were two gendarmes at the Morne Rouge station, a tall black man with a face like a mask and a short balding white man with a mustache and an air of melodrama about him. All the two appeared to have in common was their uniform: khaki bermuda shorts and knee socks, which looked equally absurd on both of them, although in different ways.

The white officer paced back and forth across the room as if it were the operations headquarters for the Allied command in North Africa. His black deputy stood immobile, hands folded behind his back.

"Are you sure this individual has fallen into a crevasse?" asked the white officer after we told our story. "Perhaps he took another route down."

"There is no other route," said the deputy.

"Hair color? Distinguishing marks?"

I gave a detailed description.

"You said he's Italian?"

"No. Judging by his accent, Dutch or German. We

spoke in English."

"Hmmm. An Italian." He carefully wrote it down. "Blond hair."

"I told you—*Dutch or German* and *brown* hair."

"About your height, then? How old are you?"

And so it continued, insanely. The commandant recorded the "facts" like an author who changes names and faces to protect the innocent. By the time Luci and I returned to the mayor's house, the whole episode seemed more ludicrous by the minute.

The mayor didn't believe us when we first told him the story, but he played along as if it was all a splendid joke.

"What kind of scream was it?" he asked with a mischievous grin.

"Well, like the sound of a man falling to his death," I said. "You know, a scream at the movies. A man going over a cliff."

"Give me an example."

"No."

"Come on, please!"

"No, I can't."

"You must."

"Okay. *Aaaaaaaaaiiiiiiiiiiiihhhhhhhhh!*"

"No! You're joking!"

We both collapsed laughing. The mayor assured us this was the funniest thing he'd heard all year. Only Luci was able to maintain some genuine concern for this poor stranger who had fallen into a hole. But by this point I was sincerely hoping the fellow was dead, if only to be done with the business once and for all. Besides, if he was definitely dead, we would feel less ridiculous.

Luci retired to her bedroom below the mayor's apartment.

"Why don't you go with her?" said the mayor with a wink. "I'll call over my whore."

When I entered the room, Luci's eyes were closed, but I could tell that she was awake, waiting to be surprised. The moonlight had turned her cropped blond hair bluish silver. I undressed and slid under the covers. Her warmer body stoked mine, devoured it until we both came, simultaneously, our orgasms a dumb coincidence of her misguided passion and my detachment.

The next minute she was asleep and snoring. Wide awake, I focused on the window and listened to the sounds of the rainforest. They were unusually acute. Back in Guadeloupe I thought I had become accustomed to this ritual, the animal song that starts at sunset, first with crickets filling the air with layer on layer of rhythm, then with a few perfunctory tree frogs, who chirp at slow intervals until one suddenly doubles the tempo and they all jump in, pushing from one crescendo to the next like demented drums around the fire.

But there was something deliberate about the sounds that night. They conspired with Luci's ragged breathing to make peace of mind impossible. If I tried ignoring them, whenever my consciousness found a quiet corner, the jungle would sneak up and reinsinuate itself from behind. Meanwhile, the violence of Luci's snoring escalated until she was a demonic presence beside me. It subsided only when I held her and breathed in unison. I tried to lull myself to sleep this way, listening to the pulse of the forest and cradling Luci with my hand pressed against her breast—nothing else would calm her—but each time I started to drift off, a shift in the rhythms outside the window would jolt me awake.

The jungle has a jealous mind, leaving room for no other. It mocks any notions of privacy or sanity. The windowpane, as a formal barrier between inside and outside, is laughable. It is no defense against a force that slides along psychic threads, drawing a methodical web around soul and spirit.

I closed my eyes and gave in to claustrophobia, swam with the current. Letting the hallucinations have their way, I saw my mind swallowed up by black wells that collapsed endlessly into one another. Then I felt the vortex move, with a will of its own, from my head down to my chest, where it closed in around my heart, wrapped it in pain. I saw my heart encircled by the black spines of sea urchins. I saw it shrink in panic and scream inward until it was reduced to the size of a pinhole. Then, just before this tiny vestige of uninvaded identity also disappeared, it echoed with a long, hideous sound: the unmistakable sceam of the tourist.

A VIEW

A POSTCARD from New Mexico was waiting for me when I got back to Toronto.

Hot sand and navaho waves. Love the desert. A beach in the shape of the sky. Nicole drives, I navigate. We've got a big old dusty Buick that only gets AM. No air con. Dreams of *Dolores toute nue dans ma Tornado.* Plan to go through California, up to Montana and back east across the prairies. Saw *Last Tango* again at a rep theater in Albuquerque. Better the second time. Love, Cléo.

Nicole was an old friend of Cléo's, tall and angular with Oz-green eyes and masses of orange hair. I tried to picture them cruising through the southern states, talking French in truck stops and dissecting the men who would pretend not to stare. I gazed at Cléo's handwriting, the perfect petite scrunched-up script, and pondered the word before the signature: *love.* For a second all the old feelings came rushing back, converging on a glimmer of romantic possibility. I wondered what it would be like after all this time, then dismissed the whole idea with a shiver.

The summer passed anti-climactically, as summers do in Toronto, humid windless days piling up like traffic. I freelanced for magazines and started seeing someone, a smart blonde with a disarming sense of humor. She was a writer too. She had a bed with forest-green sheets, an amazing body, and liked nothing better than the idea of a northern lake. In fact, she seemed perfect in every way, although she couldn't figure out what she was doing with a man who had absolutely no interest in the future. She kept saying I wasn't all there, and wondered if it was worth waiting around to see if the rest of me would ever come into focus. As far as I was concerned, my sanity had cleared its probation period. But she claimed I was still distracted.

Cléo was living alone in Montreal, back in the same apartment on Hutchison Street. She had given up painting and begun to write fiction. I went to visit her once. I flew instead of taking the train—hardly anybody takes the train anymore. It was late September and the leaves had begun to turn. The third-floor apartment looked much the same, the afternoon sun streaming through the dust in the bedroom window. Cléo and I sat across the old table in the kitchen, with the fire-escape door open to the breeze and the sounds of kids echoing up from the courtyard. She made strong coffee on the gas stove with one of those small steel espresso pots.

Mostly she talked and I interviewed, which was the way it used to be. I was always grateful for her ability to talk. It relieved the pressure. Sitting with her, for a moment I felt we were back there, living together again in our separate worlds. It occurred to me that we never had the casual symmetry that people need to spend their lives together. There was always something vaguely illicit about us, a passion heightened by the premonition of its demise. We knew it would never last, even in the early days. I remember we were painting the apartment together, rolling the walls white, "No Expectations" came on the radio. With that line about our love being like the water that flashes on a stone. We were nostalgic before it was over, not for each other so much, but for the time.

Later that afternoon, we went to a book fair to hear a friend of a former comrade read from a volume of poetry, her first. The event took place in the lobby of the newspaper where I used to work. But the paper had moved to a newer building with picture windows on the ground floor that let you see the printing presses from the sidewalk.

The poet was in the middle of reading a remarkable verse about killing a fish when I felt a tap on my shoulder. I didn't recognize him at first, but it was Conrad, the reporter who had taken over my job after I'd quit the paper. He was on his way up to work, and he asked me to drop by later if I had a moment.

After the reading, I left Cléo at the book fair and rode the elevator up to the newsroom. It was a Saturday, and the place was deserted. I found Conrad sitting alone at the police desk, behind a glass booth overlooking a room of empty desks and computer terminals. He was eating a ham sandwich and writing a story about English-language rights.

"It's nothing," he said. "A piece of ten-inch filler. You want a tour?"

He took me around the office and we talked about how much newsrooms had changed. I reminisced about the clatter of manual typewriters, the loud suck of the pneumatic tube next to my head as copy boys sent stories to the composing room, the rush of writing on deadline and passing the yellow pages one at a time to the city desk, to Frank who sat there like a coach, yelling, "Bang it out, just keep banging it out," as he penciled his way through the copy.

Returning to the police desk, Conrad talked about his divorces and the way we used to do drugs and how Montreal had lost its excitement.

"It's not the same," he said. "People are too serious. I think they're depressed."

"What, about the politics?"

"It's all bullshit. Total bullshit. But what can you do?"

"How about the paper?"

"It's a job. I've worked a lot of places and they're not that different. This one's okay." He took a bite of his sandwich, something thin and pale from a vending machine. He chewed slowly. "Would you like some?"

"No, thanks."

"Sure?"

"I'm fine."

It was eerie, sitting there with Conrad and his sandwich behind the glass, staring out over an empty newsroom, a lame fluorescent light twitching in the corner. I imagined myself in his place. I could feel the moment expanding around us, like an anesthetic.

"Whatever happened to that girl you were with?" asked Conrad.

"What girl?"

"Weren't you with some French girl?"

"Cléo. I came with her. She's downstairs."

"Really, you're still together?"

"No, we're just friends."

That evening Cléo and I went to the book-launch party. A lot of the old faces were there. The Organization had splintered into groupuscules, and most of the former members were no longer active. Except Marcel, who continued to work with what was left of the International, arranging documents for political refugees and serving as a contact for Latin American comrades involved in anti-fascist resistance movements. He looked much the same: the graying beard stained with nicotine, the eyes weary with political intelligence but still sparking with wit. Marcel always made communism seem credible and dignified. He didn't really voice opinions. He would describe the latest development in the class struggle with loving precision, as if it were standing right there in front of him, like a building, and he was a dedicated draftsman sketching all its angles and contours in irrefutable detail. It was better in French, though. A phrase like "*le rapport des forces dans la conjoncture actuelle*" sounded much sexier than "the relationship of forces in the current period."

Marcel regaled a couple of friends with the story of my final days at the newspaper. For him, my relationship with the labor minister had taken on legendary status: the fable of the Marxist and the Machiavellian. The way Marcel told it, I had practically infiltrated the Quebec cabinet, a Trotskyist double-agent who became the minister's confidant. He talked about how the two of us, the journalist and the politician, played both ends against the middle on a tightrope of realpolitik, and how we both fell from grace in the tumult of the James Bay sabotage—the Machiavellian losing his ministry, the Marxist losing his mind.

"We sent him to Toronto." Marcel grinned. "We didn't know what the hell to do with him. So we thought we'd let the Toronto comrades handle it."

"But you played along with my delusions," I said.

"What else could we do? Have you locked up? You were on Mars. Do you remember when you phoned me from Toronto at four in the morning?"

"No."

"You woke me up and said, 'People here think I'm crazy.' I said, 'It's the middle of the fucking night. You *are* crazy.'"

It was a mild evening. I walked Cléo home, up the Esplanade with its curving staircase apartments. Across the slanted park, we could see the dark outline of the Mountain, a cuticle moon above the cross. Walking up the broad sidewalks of Parc Avenue, past the all-night Greek joints, we stopped by the Bagel Factory. Standing in line, we watched the bakers slice and knead Plasticine rings out of the dough, sliding them in and out of the oven on long wooden paddles. The baker working the fire, who had been there forever, said hello to me but didn't notice Cléo standing next to me. He asked the same question he would always ask when I used to come there.

"You and Cléo still together?"

Cléo poked her head out.

"You married?"

"No."

"You should get married. Anyone together that long should get married."

The next day I walked to the Mountain. There was a group of hand drummers playing by the statue overlooking Parc Avenue. A dozen drummers led by Africans. I stopped to watch for a while, itching to join in, then moved on. I hadn't intended to go to the top, but I followed the road that angles up the side, eventually cutting up through the woods on one of the squirrelly footpaths leading to the summit. There was the usual scattering of tourists ringed around the stone wall at the promontory, kids climbing up on the swivel binoculars, people taking pictures.

I looked over the ledge, noticing the line where the stone merged with the steep hillside, and thought of Scilla, of my days spent on the parapet distilling vectors from the wind, scanning the sea for waterspouts. Nothing synchronizes the scheme of things like a good view. The details shrink away, leaving a unified design, a palette of shadow and wind. But that afternoon the air was still. A vague drone of traffic drifted up from the city, which unwrinkled from the base of the Mountain like coral from a cliff. I scanned the downtown, trying to decipher streets and buildings, then focused blankly on the white cross of Place Ville Marie. There was a haze in the air, a watercolor wash that sapped the color out of everything. In the distance you could see the flat gleam of the river. To the east, I picked out the circumflex curves of the Jacques Cartier Bridge. I stared at the bridge for quite a while, half expecting it to do something, then thought it was time to go back down.

This book is set in Garamond, a standard typeface used by book designers and printers for four centuries, and one of the finest old styles ever cut. Some characteristics of Garamond to note are the small spur on the "G," the open bowl on the "P," the curving tail on the "R," and the short lower-case height and very small counters of the "a" and "e."

The text stock is
55 lb. Windsor High-bulk Cream